To Do: A Book of Alphabets and Birthdays

TO DO

A Book of Alphabets and Birthdays

BY GERTRUDE STEIN

With Illustrations by
Giselle Potter
and an Introduction by
Timothy Young

Yale University Press,
New Haven and London
in association with
Beinecke Rare Book and
Manuscript Library

yalebooks.com

Designed by Margaret Bauer
Set in Quadraat. Printed in
Hong Kong by Sing Cheong
Printing Co. Ltd.

**Library of Congress
Cataloguing-in-Publication Data**

Stein, Gertrude, 1874–1946.
To do: a book of alphabets and
birthdays / Gertrude Stein; with
illustrations by Giselle Potter and an
introduction by Timothy Young.
p. cm.
ISBN 978-0-300-17097-9
(cloth: alk. paper)
I. Potter, Giselle. II. Title

PS3537.T323T6 2011
813'.52—dc22   2010052431

A catalogue record for this book is
available from the British Library.

This paper meets the require-
ments of ANSI / NISO Z39.48–1992
(Permanence of Paper).

10 9 8 7 6 5 4 3 2 1

Jacket illustration by Giselle Potter

Introduction

TIMOTHY YOUNG

WE ALL HAVE birthdays, and we all know the alphabet. Gertrude Stein understood this to be true, and so she wrote *To Do: A Book of Alphabets and Birthdays.* But before Stein wrote *To Do,* she did a lot of other things.

Gertrude Stein was born in Allegheny, Pennsylvania, on February 3, 1874. She was raised principally in Oakland, California, attended the Harvard Annex, and then spent two years at Johns Hopkins Medical School. In 1903 she joined her brother, Leo, in Paris, where she remained for the rest of her life. In Paris, Stein focused on writing, on her admiration and support for artists such as Pablo Picasso and Juan Gris, and on her love for Alice Toklas, with whom she shared a home and a life for nearly forty years.

Owing to its cubist techniques, Stein's writing proves challenging to many readers. Her style evolved over time from the comparatively straightforward *Three Lives* (1909) and *Tender Buttons* (1914)

to her hermetic period in the 1920s, exemplified by *Stanzas in Meditation.* Her breakthrough to popular readership occurred with *The Autobiography of Alice B. Toklas* (1933), a delightful memoir of her early days in Paris. This was followed by *Everybody's Autobiography* (1937), a travelogue of her 1934–35 visit to the United States, in which she recounts many anecdotes, such as meeting Charlie Chaplin at a Hollywood party.

Stein wrote her first children's book in 1938. Commissioned by William R. Scott for his eponymous publishing company, *The World Is Round* was one of the first titles in a new publishing venture based on the innovative teaching methods of the Bank Street School in New York. It was an experiment to see how Stein's writing would be received by children, and the project was successful. *The World Is Round,* a tale of how little Rose climbed mountains and learned about lions, appeared in 1939 with illustrations by Clement Hurd (best known today for the images he created for *Good-night Moon*) and has been reprinted several times and published in multiple languages. Many critics praised *The World Is Round*, stating that Stein had finally found her true audience. Feeling confident in this success, Stein decided to write a second book for children.

Stein sent the manuscript for *To Do: A Book of Alphabets and Birthdays* to William R. Scott in the spring of 1940. Scott rejected the manuscript, stating that the book was not appropriate for children. This view was confirmed by rejections from other publishers and by friends who read the manuscript, including Carl Van Vechten (who nonetheless worked tirelessly to find a publisher for the work). Margaret Wise Brown, who published many books with William R. Scott, wrote to Stein to praise the book, and Stein persevered to find a home for it. After another year of rejections, Stein was finally offered a contract in March 1942 by Harrison Smith, the successful publisher of the English-language editions of the Babar series in the 1930s. Although letters to Van Vechten from the literary agent who placed the book (Margot Johnson of Ann Watkins, Inc.) mention that Smith had chosen an illustrator, the identity is never revealed in the correspondence, nor does Stein's original contract survive. According to Bruce Kellner's *Gertrude Stein Companion*, Stein had envisioned her friend Raoul Dufy as the book's illustrator. In September 1943, Johnson wrote to Van Vechten to report that *To Do* was postponed because of problems with the illustrations. Further delays, likely caused by the economic realities of wartime, effectively canceled the project.

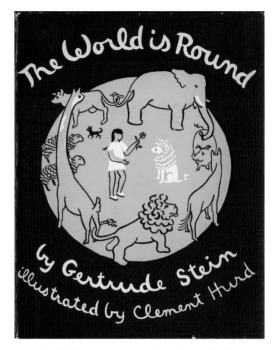

Jacket, *The World is Round* by Gertrude Stein, illustrated by Clement Hurd (New York: William R. Scott, 1939). Yale Collection of American Literature, Beinecke Rare Book and Manuscript Library

Gertrude Stein with a teletype machine during her U.S. tour, 1934–35. Gertrude Stein and Alice B. Toklas Papers, Yale Collection of American Literature, Beinecke Rare Book and Manuscript Library

To Do was first published (without illustrations) in 1957 by Yale University Press, in the seventh volume of the *Yale Edition of the Unpublished Writings of Gertrude Stein*, a project overseen by Donald Gallup, longtime curator of the Gertrude Stein and Alice B. Toklas Papers. The present edition, illustrated by Giselle Potter, is the first publication of the text with images. Potter's witty and stylish illustrations provide a perfect complement to Stein's uniquely whimsical world of words.

Readers might wonder whether any of the characters in *To Do* are based on real people. After all, Stein is known to have incorporated and even to have created entire works based on stories from the lives of her friends. So, are the boys and girls, men and women, dogs and goats, and measles and allergies in this book based on real life? Some are.

— George [Platt Lynes] was a photographer, and he had prematurely gray hair.

— Katy Buss was a journalist from Massachusetts and a friend of Stein's.

— Robert, or Bobolink, was Robert Bartlett Haas, a young scholar from California who was working with Donald Gallup in the early 1940s on a bibliography of Stein's writings. He did, in fact, postpone his wedding due to a case of measles.

— Sammy, the boy who could not eat birthday cake but could eat the candles, was Sam Steward — a novelist, teacher, and, later, famous tattoo artist who had pronounced allergies.

— Tillie Brown was a childhood friend of Stein's. Tillie's story companion, Thornie Rose, is modeled after Thornton Wilder, the novelist and playwright and close friend of Stein's. Like Brown, Wilder was a child of missionaries.

— Papa Woojums was Carl Van Vechten ("Van"), and Alice Toklas was Mama Woojums and Gertrude Stein was Baby Woojums.

The balance of quartets of children, adults, and animals — wistful, playful, and sometimes doomed — are as real or as fictional as the protagonists in works by other modern writers such as Ernest Hemingway or Alfred Jarry.

In *To Do*, birthdays are as mutable as language for Stein. Characters question what day is their birthday; they want to change the dates of their birthdays; they don't want to share them. One can easily appreciate the view of Stein's friends and potential publishers: children are not the core audience for this book. In addition to the challenging linguistic exercises, there is a recurrent sense of menace in some of the stories: children drown while swimming across a river; a group of forty dogs tears up everyone they meet; a soldier loses an eye in battle; a rabbit self-immolates! On the other hand, this sort of danger and unpleasantness is certainly also found in the European children's folklore tradition. Stein's untimely demises are gentle compared to the often brutal climaxes in the tales of Jacob and Wilhelm Grimm or even Edward Gorey.

As for the grammar of the book, one needs to appreciate the essential role of abstraction. Abstraction permits us to play with language, form, and images: to color outside the lines and then to move the lines to capture the liberated color. Stein is our great example of how modern writers experimented with language by setting aside the constraints of grammar, punctuation, and linear narrative in search of new forms of expression. But to read her is to see that she is, in some ways, conservative. She uses words familiar to our eyes and ears, and, if we punctuate by learned habit, her sentences flow into stories that have structure. The use of repetition in her writing, one of Stein's most famous traits, works to reinforce action, dialogue, and characteristics. When we speak, it is natural to stop and start, truncate, begin again, repeat, trail off…Stein had a gift for capturing the flow of spoken language as written narrative. In the press release for *The World Is Round*, Stein provided a statement for her readers: "Don't bother about the commas which aren't there, read the words. Don't worry about the sense that is there, read the words faster. If you have any trouble, read faster and faster until you don't." For Stein, composition was explanation—the writing was the meaning.

What "to do" with this book, then? Read it out loud, slowly at first, then speed it up, as Stein suggested. Read the funniest parts to a child. They won't question the grammar a bit. Then read it to yourself. Stop and start. Then, when someone has a birthday, choose a page at random and read it to her. Because everyone knows the alphabet and everyone has a birthday.

First page of Gertrude Stein's handwritten manuscript of *To Do: A Book of Alphabets and Birthdays*, 1940. Gertrude Stein and Alice B. Toklas Papers, Yale Collection of American Literature, Beinecke Rare Book and Manuscript Library

To Do:
A Book of Alphabets
and Birthdays

GERTRUDE STEIN

ALPHABETS and names make games and everybody has a name and all the same they have in a way to have a birthday.

The thing to do is to think of names.

Names will do.

Mildew.

And you have to think of alphabets too, without an alphabet well without names where are you, and birthdays are very favorable too, otherwise who are you.

Everything begins with A .

What did you say. I said everything begins with A and I was right and hold me tight and be all right.

Everything begins with A.

A. Annie, Arthur, Active, Albert.

Annie is a girl Arthur is a boy Active is a horse. Albert is a man with a glass.

Active.

Active is the name of a horse.

Everybody has forgotten what horses are.

What horses are.

What are horses.

Horses are animals were animals with a mane and a tail ears hoofs a head and teeth and shoes if they are put upon them.

If they are put upon them and then the horses lose them and if any one finds them and keeps them, he has lots of good luck. But now everybody has forgotten what horses are and what horse-shoes are and what horse-shoe nails are everybody has forgotten what horses are, but anyway one day, Active is the name of a horse, a nice horse.

He had a birthday he was born on that day so everybody knew just how old he was, he was born on the thirty-first of May on that day, and then he began to say he was not born on that day he was he began to say he was born on the thirty-first of June, and that was none too soon. He liked to be born later every day. Well anyway, there he was and Active was his name, it was his name now but it had not always been, it had once been Kiki, not that he ever kicked not he and he used then to pull a milk-wagon. Then the war came, Kiki was twenty, twenty is awful old for a horse but Kiki had always had plenty, so even at twenty he was young and tender and pretty slender.

So the soldiers came along and they thought he was young and strong and they took him along and everybody was crying and the milk was drying, but they did take Kiki along and he was he was old but he was young and strong.

Then nobody knew where he was, and he was no he was not gone away nor did he stay but he was at the front where there was shooting and he was pulling a little cannon along, and they did not know his name but he was so young and strong they called him Active and he always came right along he and his little cannon. And somebody wrote to him and he answered I have a very nice man, and they sent the very nice man chocolate and everything so he would give Active some, and he did and everybody liked everything even the little cannon that Active was pulling. That is the way it was. And so Active went right along and some one said to him if you make believe you are not well they will send you home. Can I take my little cannon said Active I like it better than a milk-wagon, I like being Active better than Kiki who was never kicking. I guess I will stay where I am, Active was answering.

And so it went on, and one day there was no more fighting everything was calm, Active was quiet and warm and everybody was going home. And Active was sent home to the milk-wagon, and the milk-wagon was changed to an automobile and they did not need Active for that, they could only use him for ploughing, and they called him Kiki again but Active was his name and he said he would lose his mane if they took away his new name. Well they all cried like anything, they just all cried and cried and then Active forgot everything and he said ploughing was not so bad, and he could always be glad, and anyway, what

was the use of saying anything since everybody did what they pleased with him. So he said he thought an automobile, just one day he said he thought he would be an automobile not a new one an old one and he was one, he was an automobile and an automobile never has a name and it never has a mane and it has rubber shoes not an iron one and finding rubber shoes does not mean anything like finding iron horse-shoes did and that was the end of everything.

Then there is B. Well Annie did get mixed up with B. but naturally enough if you see that B follows A and A comes before B.

B is for Bertha and Bertie and Ben and Brave and a birthday for each one.

B is for Bertha the one who was the mother of some children. There were three of them.

Bertie was cross-eyed because somebody when he was a baby always stroked his nose with their finger.

The second was Ben who never said when because saying it made him feel funny and the third was named Brave and Brave was always white with delight.

And so each one had to have one one birthday, nobody not any one can say they just each one did not have to have a birthday, even their mother Bertha had to have one.

B for Bertha and Bertie and Ben and Brave and a birthday for each one.

Brave who was always white with delight went fishing at night. He always fished at night and that was all right because he had been born in the day and Brave was a funny boy because he was not born on his birthday. Any day could be his birthday because he was not born on his birthday. And so he could fish by night and be white with delight.

That was all right.

He was a funny boy.

To be born all right and not to be born on his birthday.

He was a funny boy.

He had two dirty dogs little yellow ones with lots of hair but no care.

They were called Never Sleeps and his brother Was Asleep.

Never Sleeps and Was Asleep always went fishing with Brave at night. Never Sleeps barked all night and Was Asleep was asleep.

Brave was a rich boy. One day, it might have been his birthday because he was not born on his birthday and any day might be his birthday well one day he met the letter A which was a little girl named Annie. Annie was very pretty, anybody could say that of Annie any day and so as Annie was born on her birthday her birthday was the seventeenth of February Brave liked to look at her and so today not Annie's birthday but a day he stopped to say well Annie where are you going today. So then he went on he said you know he said I am rich and strong and you do not need to come along but I am going to give you all my money because you are just as sweet as honey. So he did, he gave her all his money and she took it away and then it was no longer day because night had come, and Brave who was always white with delight went fishing in a river that was flowing and going with all its might. Brave always fished with a light. Nobody should because that dazzles the fish and they cannot see where for the glare so it is not fair. But Brave did he fished at night with a light. And tonight, yes tonight, he was drowned at night, drowned dead at night, and Never Sleeps barked all night and Was Asleep was asleep and Annie had all his money and she spent it on honey, and Brave was never any more white with delight. And the fish could rest every night.

This is what happens when you are not born on your birthday, that is what everybody does say this is what happens when you are not born on your birthday.

Then there is C for Charlie.

Charlie is a boy whose father made chocolate candies.

They all had birthdays.

January.

Oh yes he said and he cried. If I could have a birthday when I tried.

If I could have a birthday beside, January he said January and he cried.

Which one was it.

He did not know which one it was all he knew was that his name was Silly that he had a dog called Billy and that he wished oh how he wished that his birthday, that he had a birthday, say he had a birthday, what day would he have his birthday, oh what day and then there was nothing to say just nothing to say he did not have a birthday.

The first of January.

Nobody knows why he said oh my.

But he did.

Birthday was what he said.

Anyway is what he said.

And his named is Charlie.

That is the real surprise. That, that his name is Charlie.

He did not know it. No he did not. No he did not know it but it was his name. His name was Charlie and January was his birthday, the whole month of January every day in it was his birthday.

Now you can see why he tried and why he cried. So would anybody.

It is nice to have a birthday of January because it comes soon but then again it does not come again.

Charlie had to think of everything.

And yet he could not help it, his birthday, oh dear why try to cry, his birthday, oh dear oh dear oh dear.

January, Charlie, the new moon, and glory.

Birthdays.

D is for Dora David Dove and Darling.

And their birthdays.

Dora knew birds could fly, so did David, but not Dove and Darling, Dove and Darling knew that it was not true, they knew January was taken, no birthday, and February was short no birthday and after that it was too late.

Oh dear said Dove and Darling, no birthdays, not a birthday not one single little birthday.

It is very astonishing about birthdays, some people are born on their birthdays and some are not.

Dove and Darling and they knew it and they knew everybody would know it. Oh dear.

Dove. Love. Shove.

No birthday.

Eight weight late.

No birthdays.

Darling.

Well Darling just thought it would be neat as well as sweet to have one.

All right have one, have a birthday Darling.

Darling was talking to herself. She was saying, have one have one have one.

Nobody knew what she wanted but it was a birthday, of course it was a birthday she wanted, she just had to have one.

And then she heard Dora and David and they were eating fish and they said of course they had a birthday each one had one and what is more they were born on theirs.

Dove let out a big sigh.

She said she would try

To have a birthday oh my.

And Darling said me too

I never was born never at all.

I was never born said Darling,

And Darling was all blue.

Blue is precious said Darling,

And who are you said Dove.

I never had a birthday said Darling, and just then Charlie came along and he said a whole month of birthdays all January only January it came too soon, he would just as leave have been born at noon.

Oh dear said they all

I was born too.

Not I said Dove, I was never born, oh dear and she began to cry and she began to sigh and she began to say oh my.

Well Birthdays are very favorable.

So D comes after C. Just after. C does not care whether D comes after C or not he just does not care. C is C. What difference does it make to C that D comes after C.

But D does care he cares very much that it is such that E comes after D. It makes all the difference to D that E comes after D. Sometimes D says bad words to E says don't come tagging after me, I have had enough of E, let me be. But there it is there is no use in making a fuss E is always there, it is better to be like C and not to care. But D was never very like that, he just could not help being fussed that E was always there, he just could not help being fussed D was and E well E was used to D so he said let it be, no said D no it is not B it is E it is E that I don't want there, well I don't care said E and that was the way it began and D ran and E also ran and Annie had a fan and paper began and A and B and C and D and E were ready to see that nobody came after E. But they did F came after E which was most exciting to see and they hoped it would be a race they ran or to play catch as catch can but not at all, they had to be there at call B after A and C after B and D after C and E after D and F after E. F is in after and that makes it faster. Forget me not.

And so here is E.

Nobody must forget that E follows D. Edith, Edward, Eagle and Eat. Edith was both late, she was born a month too late.

She should have been born the fifth of June and she thought that was too soon so she was born the fifth of July oh my. So everybody knew the day was wrong so they would not say she was born that day so she just had to get along and she made a song, which said, I am ahead I am ahead, for July is later than June, and the fourth of July would be too soon and here am I not in June but in July, oh my why, but of course I know why, it is because the fifth of July is the day to try to see the sky. Edith always saw the sky. It was a way she had. Others might try to see the sky but she always could even in a thick wood nothing could keep Edith from seeing the sky, and quite right too. Why not. If not. Why not.

The sky is made to look blue.

The sky is made to look pink.

The sky is made to look black.

The sky is made to look blue.

But when Edith saw the sky it was not pink or black or white or blue, Edith could look through and as she looked through she knew that green is not blue, violet is blue, yellow is not blue but black is blue. Anybody else might be confused about the colors of the sky. But not Edith. She knew why. And the reason she knew why was that she was born on the fifth of July. Birthday or not made no difference to her, she knew why the sky was blue, why the sky was pink, why the sky was black and blue. She knew.

There was no use asking her,

She would never tell.

She said for her they rang a bell

And that was because she had not been born in June which was too soon but in July on the fifth of July oh my.

And she would never tell why.

Never never never tell why.

Eat tried to tempt her to tell.

He knew how very well.

All he had to do was to say well well

And everybody knew that he had everything to do.

Eat was his name and Eat his nature

And he tried to make Edith tell.

But no not even Eat could make Edith tell.

No said Edith no.

Edward and Eagle and Eat said oh Edith tell.

No said Edith no.

And Edward and Eagle and Eat were so excited in getting Edith to tell that they did not know very well what it was they wanted Edith to tell. And did Edith know very well what they all wanted her to tell. No Edith knew she was born the fifth of July and that she could say Oh my, and that no matter how much anybody could try they could never make her tell. But what, well she forgot and so did they, but they never said What, they were so busy making her tell and she was so busy saying never never would she tell that they did not know what it was she was to tell and it was only when they heard something that was like a bell saying What What What, that they all knew that it was what they forgot, just what, well what, then what, What what What.

And so they all went to sleep and it was F. Yes it was it was F.

But nobody must forget not yet that F follows E. Francis, Fatty, Fred and Fanny.

Every time Fatty went out he saw a four-leaf clover. That was all there was to Fatty.

But there was lots more to Francis.

Francis, Francis Putz was his name; it is a funny name but it was his name all the same. He liked dogs but he was afraid of them and he liked better talking about birds.

He had a sister who was very tiny, she was only a year younger than he was and he Francis was fair size for his age but she was tiny. In that part of the

country all the cats are tiny, there are no big ones and perhaps well it had nothing to do with it of course, but she was only a year younger and her name was Fanny Lucy and she was tiny.

They could play with the ball that belonged to the dog but they could not play with the dog because they were afraid of him. They knew that Never Sleeps and his brother Was Asleep played tag, they saw them, and they knew they played pussy wants a corner, somebody told them that, but and there was no doubt about it, Francis Putz and his sister Fanny Lucy were afraid of dogs and they went on being afraid of them. They were all outside together they and the dogs but Francis and Fanny Lucy always looked away as far as they could from them. Never Sleeps was not really there, they just knew about him, and Was Asleep was taken away so they could not see him. So they settled down to play with Was Asleep's ball. Was Asleep did not mind because he preferred sticks to balls and really Francis and Fanny Lucy did not care much for balls to play with either except just to roll between their legs when they stood with their legs apart and could get somebody to roll the ball under them. Pass through the hole is what they called it. That was what they did. There were no dogs and everything was calm. Just now.

And then they came and they went past them and they went into a house, a man and then a goat and then a woman and then a dog and then the door closed.

Francis knew no one told him but he knew the name of the man and the dog and the woman and the goat and knowing their names just scared Francis. But then anything could scare Francis. He was the son of a captain and one of his grandfathers was a colonel and the other was a general and just anything could scare Francis.

Goats have no name but men have but Francis never cared what name a man had nor a dog has but a dog does have a name. Francis only remembered his own name, Francis Putz.

Francis was afraid and then he drew a deep breath and then he looked at his sister and he was glad she was tiny because then he did not have to leave her to follow after the man the goat the woman and the dog.

And then it was night.

Nobody knew how that had happened.

Nobody knew.

And it was dark.

And the little sister was not there.

Later they were to say she had walked five miles away.

And she had.

Little as she was she had.

It was dark and it was night.

Nobody knew how it had happened but it had.

It was dark and it was night and there was no light.

It was a funny country, there were mountains but they did not mount, what there really was was a lot of water, and in the middle of the water was a river.

It can happen like that.

The next day it was Friday Francis and Fanny Lucy had a little baby brother.

They sang this song.

Come fire-fly and light up baby's nose.

Come fire-fly and light up baby's nose.

Come fire-fly and light up baby's nose.

Come fire-fly and light up baby's nose.

Then they were all happy together.

Then one day it was Monday they all were lost and there was nothing to eat but grass, so they all ate grass. They knew that grass grew, they knew there were lots of kinds of grass and they did not like any kind that grew.

Well being lost always makes everything yesterday which was Sunday and so that was the end of that. But yet there were still birthdays.

Francis was born on a day that was frightful because there was an earthquake on that day. Fanny Lucy was born on a day that was awful because it was so hot butter melted, and the baby was better, he was born on a day that was wetter than any other day but still wetter is better than another day.

They none of them ever had another birthday.

And now G comes after F. What did you say I said G comes after F. Anyway it does.

G is George Jelly Gus and Gertrude.

Nobody is so rude

Not to remember Gertrude.

George knew all about thunder and lightning but he always sat down.

He sat down when he saw lightning and he sat down when he heard thunder. Not because he was afraid but because he liked to sit down.

He always sat down with a Frown.

That meant that he did not like thunder and he did not like lightning.

He liked to say he did everything as quick as lightning. He liked to say he made a noise like thunder.

That was George.

Funny the way you said thunder and lightning when it is the lightning that comes first not the thunder.

When George was a little boy he went away. Where he went away nobody can say but they never saw George again.

George had grey hair when he was a little boy but that was all right, hair can turn white in a single night and George's did. Whether that made him go away or not who can say.

Before George went away he gave his cat away. He had more than one cat but he only gave one away. That was perhaps because its name was Anyway.

Come here Any Anyway George used to say and the cat came and he followed George about and he never had any doubt that George was George.

Then George's hair turned grey and the cat Anyway began to stay away.

Anything can worry a cat and Anyway was worried by that.

If George had had another birthday everything might have been different but he had a birthday on April Fool's Day. And he cried when he was born and he said I tried not to be born on April Fool's Day and he cried anyway all day and perhaps he always cried a little every day.

Perhaps that was the reason his hair was grey because he did cry a little every day and he had been born on April Fool's Day.

Anyway he went away and before he went away he gave his cat Anyway away.

His hair was grey and he went away and he was a little boy and his hair was grey and he was born on April Fool's Day and he went away. He was a little boy and his hair was grey and he was born on April Fool's Day and he went away and before he went away he gave his cat Anyway away.

The only thing he took with him when he went away was five rich American cookies. His mother when she made rich American cookies always made twelve of them, they had eaten seven of them and that left five of them and so he took the five of them with him when he went away.

How do you do he said to himself as he went away. Very well I thank you he said to himself as he went away.

Before he had gone far away the five rich American cookies were crumbs and the birds came and took them away, from George whose hair was grey and who was born on April Fool's Day.

George was always next to nothing and he liked photographing. He could not photograph the cookies because they were gone away so he photographed thunder and lightning. First he photographed the thunder and then he photographed the lightning and then he lay down to sleep under a big tree. A big tree does not have roots like a little tree has. A big tree that grows so high that no one can put their clothes on it to dry, has no roots to it like a little tree.

It just sits on the ground but it is so big and round that nothing can shake it, even if it does go up high as high as a sky. Think of it and try, a fat boy is harder to shake than a thin boy and George was a thin boy so he shook, he always shook just like a running brook, he shook and shook, that was the reason the rich American cookies crumbled away, that is the reason his hair was grey, that was the reason he was born on April Fool's Day that was the reason he went away and that was the reason he gave his cat Anyway away. He was so thin he was always shaking, and so he went to sleep where the biggest tree that ever grew would be sure to, not to shake. Not even in an earthquake.

Poor George, it was inch by inch that he slept, and he was not even wet, he shook so that no rain could drop on him and he shook so that he was so thin that he could never have a twin.

But let it never be forgotten that he liked branches on trees that were rotten, he was so thin they could not fall upon him, his hair was grey because he was so thin and he went away because nobody could find him he was so thin and he loved thunder and lightning because he was so thin, they could do nothing to him, and so he grew thinner and thinner and his hair grew greyer and greyer and the big tree grew bigger and bigger and three times three made twenty oftener and oftener and the lightning and the thunder grew stronger and louder and the cat Anyway was dead anyway and the rich American cookies were far away, the birds had taken them away and what could George do or say, he could take one photograph a day but that was not enough to pay his way, he had no way to pay, poor George poor dear thin George poor dear thin grey-haired George poor George he was away there is nothing more to say poor dear thin grey-haired George he was a thin grey-haired boy and he had no toy and he had no joy and the lightning and thunder were brighter and louder and the big tree was bigger and he was thinner and pretty soon well pretty soon, there was no noon there never is if you are born on April Fool's Day, there is no noon no noon, and pretty soon and in every way George dear George began to fade away, fade fade away, he was born on April Fool's Day, he was grey, he was thin he went away he knew all about lightning and thunder he was under the biggest of big trees and that was no wonder, George George it was no wonder lightning and thunder George born on April Fool's Day had faded away.

After G is H for Henry.

Henry and Harold and Henrietta and House.

Harold was the last of the Saxon kings.

Henriette de Dactyl, Yetta from Blickensdorfer and Mr. House.

Henriette was a French typewriter Yetta was a German typewriter and Mr. House was an American typewriter and they all lived together, they click clacked together only Mr. House made the least noise.

They were all three machines and they worked every day and they had nothing to say and that was the way it was.

Nature never sleeps.

That is what the little machine the typewriter Henriette de Dactyl said to herself nature never sleeps, but said Henriette de Dactyl I am not nature because whenever they let me alone I sleep, I can always sleep, I wish I could cook cookies, I wish I could plant trees, I wish I could cook mutton chops, I wish I lived on an avenue of cauliflowers I wish I wish said Henriette de Dactyl and then it went click clack and it said nature never sleeps, and it was asleep. Yetta von Blickensdorfer said I am nature because I sleep with one eye one eye one eye, said Yetta von Blickensdorfer and if you only sleep with one eye you can never cry.

These two typewriters were very little ones you could carry them around and Yetta von Blickensdorfer was very proud when they carried her around, she always kept one eye open when they carried her around, even when they put her on a high shelf she never lost herself she always kept one eye open even when the closet door was shut.

Henriette de Dactyl was not like that, she said nature never sleeps but a sweet Henriette de Dactyl sleeps very well, she too would like to live somewhere but she did not want to live on a cauliflower avenue, she wanted to live on Melon Street, and she wanted to eat radishes and she wanted to eat salads and she wanted to eat fried fish and soup. And when they carried her around and as she was a very little machine she was bound to be carried around she always closed both eyes very tight and she always let out little squeaks with all her might, and then she always hoped there would be some light if they put her on a shelf but if there was no light she said it was just right, right without moonlight and she just fell asleep both eyes shut tight.

But Mr. House he was not a mouse he was a great big typewriter, they could not carry him around, they could only cover him over.

That is what made him such a nice lover. They could not carry him around but they could just cover him over.

And so Henriette de Dactyl and Yetta von Blickensdorfer up on their shelf so high both thought they would die if they never saw Mr. House again. They knew they would, and Henriette cackled like a hen, she knew she would die if she did not try to see Mr. House the American typewriting machine again. And Yetta would groan and would moan and she knew she would be like a stone if she never could see never never never could see Mr. House the big typewriting machine again.

And so there they were and everywhere there was no one, and so would they could they did they can they will they shall they sha'n't they can't they might they if they, as they, suddenly they heard a voice say, as you were and there they were as they were.

Terrible terrible day, to be as they were.

Nature never sleeps said Henriette.

Forget forget said Mr. House

Not yet said Yetta.

And then she felt better.

But Henriette knew and Mr. House too that when the cock crew and the mouse said mew it would be Sunday.

Well very well Monday comes after Sunday.

Gracious me said Henriette, I have not been born yet.

Mr. House said in a solemn voice typewriting machines are not born they are made, and even if they are always in the shade, they are made.

Oui oui, said Henriette oui oui.

Ja ja said Yetta ah.

And Mr. House said nothing more, because he was not a bore and he would have been of course he would have been if he had said anything more.

More More More.

Shut oh shut the door.

It is shut said Henriette.

Not yet said Yetta.

And so the three typewriting machines went to war, they said they would, they would they said.

Henriette fell off the shelf.

Yetta was left there all by herself.

Mr. House quick as a mouse heard the noise, he did not go to help because he thought he heard a yelp and he did, but it was not a fuss, Henriette had fallen off the shelf but she was not a muss, she just said she would fuss and she did, and Mr. House quick as a mouse covered her with his cloth he had one of course it covered him over and so there they were Mr. House and Henriette and it was fair that they were there, and Yetta all alone on her shelf could not take care of herself, she just got dirty and cried and when anyone tried to make her keys go they stuck ever so, and so no, no there was no use, no use in that, she might as well have been a cat, and Mr. House got on very well and so did Henriette who loved to look well when they said she would tell how to fall off a shelf and not hurt herself much, it was such fun to tell every one.

So there it was begun and it was finished before they were done and every one has a gun and no one can run and that is what war is and now there is none, thank you every one.

And I follows H, it does not sound right but it is H and then ╱ it is better to try H and then I, H I makes high.

▌ is Inca Isaac Irresistible and Inez.

Isaac said that he was better, but was he. Isaac said that he felt better but did he. Isaac said that children should be seen and not heard but should they. Isaac said that eighty was more than four but is it. Isaac said that ink is blacker than blue but is it. Isaac said that bridges are wetter than clouds but are they. Isaac said that water is wetter than dolls but is it, Isaac said that yes is quicker than no but is it. Isaac said that butter is whiter than snow but is it. Isaac said that leaves are red, but are they; Isaac said that he had read that he would be dead if he went away, and said what he had said but would he. Isaac said that it was better to be red than blue but is it. Isaac said that a clock would stop if you said what what, but would it. Isaac said that he met a head and when he met a head he hit it, but did he. Isaac said that he changed what he said so that it came back to sit with it, but did it. Isaac said that a chance to wed would come if he saw some one, but did it. Isaac said that it was all right that he would stay awake every night but would he. Isaac said that he felt like lead, but did he. Isaac said that when he ran he always began but did he. Isaac said not at all, not at all, and then Isaac said everything is all everything is all and Isaac said I am very tall but is he.

J comes after I of course it does, it was of course it was ⌡. Jay, Jay is a bird, a bird that if it comes it eats green peas and little thumbs. Of course it comes, it is grey and black and wishes it was all black because nobody would know it was back but of course I was thinking of a magpie. But ⌡ is other things it is James, Jonas, Jewel and Jenny, and anybody can ask more.

But and there must always be more than one there must always be four,

no more, just four. J is also just, just why, that is no lie, just why or why, well well.

But after all well well and you can never tell if it is a bell or if it is just well well. Well anyway, I does come before J. It is no lie, it does it just does come before J even if there is a J to pay and there is in just, not in must but in just.

So then to say that I comes before J remember I is Ivy.

Ivy was Ivy, she was Ivy by name and Ivy by nature and she was born on the fifth of August, what a lovely day to have as a birthday, the fifth of August, it is so warm it is never cold and nobody ever needs to be told that it is cold because it never is cold.

And so Ivy was Ivy by name and Ivy by nature and she was warm like August and small and round like 5, and there she was and what happened to her. Well she fell in love with a king. He was such a pretty king and so she fell in love with him.

There is no use in being a pretty king if a king is a pretty king well there is no such thing.

And so Ivy fell in love with a pretty king and really there is no such thing.

But she did she fell in love with a pretty king and he was king and she was in love with him and he was pretty and she was in love with him.

So she said she would sit at home and be in love with a pretty king. And she did she sat at home and she was in love with a pretty king. And it was everything and he was pretty and he was a king and she stayed at home and she was in love with him.

And he came to see her yes he did and he said here I am and she said yes, and he said here I am all the time and she said yes, and he said I am a king and she said yes and she said yes and such a pretty king.

Well up to then he had known he was a king but he had not known that he was such a pretty king. And now she said yes and such a pretty king. Then every one said yes and such a pretty king and then some one said should a king be a pretty king should a king be such a pretty king and soon every one was saying should a king they were saying should a king be a pretty king should a king be such a pretty king, and Ivy said yes, and everybody else said no and the king did not say anything no king ever does, and so one day well it did happen one day he was not a king and he went and saw Ivy who was sitting and he said I am not a king, and she said and such a pretty king, and he said such a pretty king and she said such a pretty king and so they said let us sit down and they sat and Ivy said yes such a pretty king and the king said yes and Ivy said yes and they both breathed tenderness and it was the fifth of August and very warm and it was the day Ivy had been born and it was her birthday and the king did not have one, he had had one when he was a king but now he was not a king he did not have one. But anyway Ivy had one, and when two are one then one is one, and Ivy and the king had begun and they never knew that two are one and the only thing they knew was that the fifth of August was warm. Which of course it is.

And so H. I. J. you have to say h i j to be sure that J comes after I which it does.

There were two brothers and two sisters James, Jonas, Jewel and Jenny, they used to quarrel about which was the biggest, they used to quarrel about which was the oldest they used to quarrel about which was the tallest they used to quarrel about which was the smallest and when they quarreled they used to say that they would take away each other's birthday. And they did that was just what they did, just exactly what they did.

One day each one had taken away somebody else's birthday and at the end of the day not one of the four of them had a birthday, they had everything to say but they just did not at the end of the day they just did not any one of them they just did not have a birthday.

And now they wondered what they should do. There was no use being in a stew, each one had taken the birthday away from the other one and now all four of them had none, because each one as soon as they had taken the other's birthday away they had thrown it away and later on when they all wanted their birthdays back again they went out to find them but they were gone perhaps a duck or a lobster had eaten them anyway all four birthdays were gone not one of them had one.

So they decided to advertise, they said they would pay to have any one give them their birthday back again or if not that one then some other one. But it was funny nobody answered them there evidently were none, no birthdays to give away, and so James and Jonas and Jewel and Jenny had none between all four of them they did not have a single one.

And then they remembered they had heard of them there were the dogs Never Sleeps and Was Asleep perhaps while Never Sleeps was barking and Was Asleep was asleep they might take their birthdays away from them. And they did, they went up very carefully while Never Sleeps was barking and Was Asleep was asleep and they took their birthdays away from them. And really Never Sleeps and Was Asleep would not mind much not even when they found that their birthdays were gone, but and that was another thing, there were four of them James, Jonas, Jewel and Jenny and there were only two birthdays for the four of them and they quarreled more than before and pretty soon they tore the two birthdays in pieces and now there were six without birthdays James and Jonas and Jewel and Jenny and Never Sleeps and Was Asleep and six without birthdays is just six too many.

What was there to do.

And then they were all so tired they lay down to sleep all except Never Sleeps and Was Asleep, that of course, and when they slept they dreamed they dreamed that across a wide river perhaps it was the Mississippi and it was a mile deep there were birthdays to give away every day and so all four, James and

Jonas and Jewel and Jenny started to swim across to where birthdays were no loss, of course Never Sleeps and Was Asleep did not try to cross and as they tried to swim across all four were drowned, of course they were drowned they had no birthdays so of course they were drowned and Never Sleeps' and Was Asleep's sleep was sound and the birthdays were never found there were none of them around. And this is the end of a sad story.

So after J comes K. K is easily K, it looks different it is different it is K. K is Kiki, Katy, Cake and Kisses.

Mrs. misses kisses

Mrs. kisses most.

Mrs. misses kisses

Mrs. kisses most.

Katy, Katy Buss

What a fuss

What a fuss

Katy Buss.

Katy Buss was her name

Katy Buss was her game

Katy Buss was her fame

Katy Buss was the same.

So there now.

How

So there now.

Katy Buss knew how to make cake.

She made it.

Katy Buss knew how to kiss

She kissed it.

Katy Buss knew Kiki Buss.

Kiki Buss knew Katy Buss

And it was ice and it was so
And it was dates and it was snow.
And then actually Katy Buss ate it.
All this sounds funny but it was money.
Money makes makes cakes.
Katy Buss sighed.
It was extraordinary how she sighed
She loved her birthday.
She just loved her birthday.
Her birthday was on the fifteenth.
After that it was on the twenty-first
And after that it was on the first.
Always the same month always the same year and that was queer.
Necessary but queer.
And now to hear
What Katy Buss has to say.
She stands on a chair which is there.
She leans on a table when she is able
She reads a book which she took
And she made it do who are you.
This is the way it does.
She said does and this was the way it was
She said me and then she put out to sea
She said very well then and she pulled all the feathers off of a hen
She said might I glide
And she knew what there was beside
And she said today yes today,
Yes today makes yesterday.
Well she said yesterday well yesterday was my birthday.

Everybody was surprised.

They well might be.

And beside

Well anyway there is enough to say and Katy Buss said it.

And there is enough to eat

And Katy Buss ate it

And there is enough to know

And Katy Buss knew it

And there is enough to chew

And Katy Buss chewed it.

Who knows what a cow does.

A cow chews its cud

Who knows what Katy Buss does.

She does and she was.

Was what

Katy Buss.

Oh dear they next to know nothing.

That was what was just as likely.

Next to know nothing.

Katy Buss went purple with joy.

Kiki Buss did it to annoy

And Klux Buss said ahoy.

Nobody came which was a shame,

And just then,

Well very likely it was just then,

Katy Buss flew, she flew right away to kiss her birthday.

For goodness' sakes is what it had to say is what her birthday had to say but Katy Buss did not mind. She was that kind, the kind that did not mind.

And it was just next to nothing

But she had her birthday,
All right she had her birthday
All right All right she had her birthday.
All right All right All right.
All right
All right she had her birthday.
And nobody said what.
And she did have it.
She had her birthday.
Which day
The first day.
And what month
The third month
And what year
Any year
Oh dear.
Remember it is queer.
It is of course
Believe it or not it is of course.
And Katy Buss could be cross
And she was.
And that is all there is to that.
L comes after K
Like it or not it does.
L is Lily-Leslie, Let and Up.
Well do you understand that.
This is the sad story of Leslie-Lily.
Lily who always found everything Hilly.
Leslie's little Lily's last birthday.

When he said come she always came
When he said go she always goes
Come come he said and she comes
Go go he said and she goes
And he says come come and she comes
And he says go go and she goes
And it worries her toes
And tickles her nose
But still when he says come come she comes
And when he says go go she goes.
And this is Leslie's Lily's last birthday.

Any hen has a birthday, it does seem funny to say it that way but any hen has a birthday any hen or any chicken or any lily, all this is peculiar.

And any hen and any chicken and any lily has its last birthday. Sometimes they say they will have their last birthday all together, the chicken eats the lily, the lily loves the hen the hen loves the chicken and they all say when and Leslie eats the chicken and the chicken said when and Leslie ate the hen and the hen said when and the lily, the tiger lily, the white lily, the purple lily, the double lily, Leslie's little lily had a last birthday and she did say when.

So it might have been but was it then, the hen was but not the chicken, Leslie was but not the lily, the lily was little and lily white and fat and that, that was what the chicken was the chicken was little and white and fat and he ate Leslie's lily and that was that. So the lily Leslie's little lily had its last birthday.

Its first birthday was hard to see because it did not show it was so slow but the last birthday was easy to see because the lily was always on the go, it hoped for snow but even so it was very easy to know.

Now when was its last birthday. Just what day.

Rather not said Leslie.

By that he meant that he would rather not that the little lily had a birthday.

He just would rather not. That is what he meant when he said rather not and he did say rather not.

But the little Lily had a birthday just the same it had no name they just called it a little lily which it was but it had no name not a real name not a name that anybody would know was a name but it had a birthday. You can have a birthday without a name and the little lily had done it it had a birthday without a name and so anybody can understand why Leslie looking down at his hand said rather not.

And then oh deary me what did Leslie see when he looked down at his hand anybody can understand what he did see when he looked down at his hand, he saw he had plucked the lily the fat little lily, the fat white little lily and he had it in his hand.

Anybody can understand.

Oh dear.

M and N are the middle of the Alphabet one one end of the middle and the other the other end of the middle and they have not the slightest idea whether they should look at each other or not. They were never ready, one looked one way the other looked the other way.

And so one way M was Marcel, Marcelle, Minnie and Martin and N was Nero, Netty, Nellie and Ned.

Well which was it said or red.

Which was it.

Well to begin.

Man is man was man will be in.

In what.

In a minute.

Just not.

Not what

Not more than a minute.

Madagascar

Please shut the better part of a half up in a car.

And that is what they meant.

I like it when they think that twenty and twenty make forty.

I do hope that you do.

So listen well.

Marcel is the name of a boy and Marcelle is the name of a girl.

It takes an eye to see that a girl has a double l e and the boy has only one l.

It does take an eye a quick eye or a slow eye but it does take an eye. An ear well an ear is good enough but it is not enough it takes an eye.

Marcel and Marcelle were going to a marrying bee. A marrying bee is where you go to see and when you see you say she will be married to me. Marcelle and Marcel had not seen each other before but when they went through the door he said she for me and she said he for me.

So then they married and they had two children Minnie and Martin.

So then there were four and when the four were there it was time something was happening.

And it did happen.

The birds began to sing

They sang like anything.

And then suddenly they stopped and sat.

And why, because they saw their first bat,

The first bat of the season

 A little black bat that was making believe it was a bird just like that.

And so the birds stopped singing and a bat can't sing

So it was the moment for Martin and Minnie to begin.

They did.

In the meantime Marcel the father and Marcelle the mother began to shudder.

It was the bat that made them feel like that the first bat of the season.

And then pretty soon Marcelle the mother and Marcel the father saw a glow-worm and that gave them quite a turn.

So everything was happening and it was evening.

Way up in the sky ever so high was something flying it was not a bird it was not a bat it was not a hat, it was an airplane and that was that.

Please Mr. Airplane take us flying said Martin and Minnie very nearly crying.

But Marcel the father said firmly no, it is better to think than to go, I tell you so.

Martin and Minnie went away they had nothing to say but they knew oh how they knew that it would happen to be true that way up high like a bird in the sky they would fly.

Papa Marcel and Mamma Marcelle had said very well, it is always necessary to say very well and Papa Marcel had been up there once too. Papa Marcel knew everything and he said enough is enough. And Mamma Marcelle knew everything and she said enough is enough but Minnie and Martin they did not know anything and so they said not enough is not enough it is all stuff, we do not know enough not enough.

And so while Mamma Marcelle and Papa Marcel were asleep and dreaming Minnie and Martin were dreaming and they were awake and they said it would be better than cake to sit and swim in the moon and to sit on the clouds and to have curtains for breakfast curtains of sky oh my they said, oh my.

They were not asleep they were dreaming and all of a sudden there it was tumbling an airplane coming and before they knew they were there. And everybody said come out quick, take an umbrella call it a fence open it quickly and down you will come in the fog that is dense and it will be like soup in a minute and later then you will be awake just a minute.

It was very likely that nothing had happened very likely, very likely indeed, it was very likely that it was Papa Marcel and Mama Marcelle who were awake and dreaming and Minnie and Martin who were asleep and dreaming, very likely. So they had the next day.

And now there was going to be a large party because it was everybody's birthday.

April eighteenth was everybody's birthday.

Everybody liked to be born on the same day so that it was more economical. If the father and the mother and the brother and the sister were born on the same day it is very much more economical, because then the birthday cake can all be made on the same day, the party can all be had on the same day, the presents can all be had on the same day, it is much more economical, and so to be economical Marcel the father and Marcelle the mother and Minnie the daughter and Martin the son were all born on that one, that one same day.

If you think this pleased every one you are mistaken.

It did not.

It did not please Minnie for one.

It did not please Martin for one.

It did not please Marcelle for one.

It did not please Marcel for one.

It did not so it would appear if you believe all you hear.

It did not please any one.

But all the same it was done, they were all born on the same day and then what happened. Well what happened what happened was this the eighteenth of April was over before they all were done being born and they were all so worn, so worn out with having been born, that when they heard the birds singing and the bat flying and the airplane whirring, they just gave up they just did, they said they were just worn out with being born, they were not going to have a party or cake or presents or anything, they were just not. And so you see it really was extremely economical because as they were all born on the same day and they were all too tired with having been born all on the same day to go on having a birthday they just did not have anything and that is very economical.

And now the first half of the alphabet is done and the second half of the alphabet is begun.

N is begun

Nero Netty Nellie and Ned.

There are twenty-six letters in the alphabet and half of twenty-six is thirteen and thirteen is an unlucky number, of course if one cannot help one's self and one is in a hurry to be born and just cannot wait until the fourteenth or if one is always a little slow and could not get born on the twelfth, there is nothing to do but just do what you do that is get born on the thirteenth, and the alphabet being twenty-six letters it has two thirteenths and you can see that they are worried about being unlucky because they got called M and N. Any one pretty well any one would know that M and N are unlucky. You have just heard the sad story of the Marcels and Marcelles and Minnies and Martins and now it is N and there is the sad story of Nero and Netty and Nellie and Ned.

It is very sad, they just could not be glad it is very sad, M is very sad and N is very sad and they just could not be glad and it was of course it was because that alphabet instead of having twenty-eight letters went to work and had twenty-six and the half of twenty-six is thirteen, and halves are always two and so all the way through N and M had to be thirteen and neither of them could be a king or a queen or a bird or a crow or a cow or a hen or a lamp or a house or a cat or a mouse, they just had to be thirteen, they could be nothing in between.

M thirteen N thirteen and thirteen is thirteen and oh dear. Who said oh dear.

Nero said oh dear and Nellie said oh dear and Netty said oh dear and Ned said oh dear and they all said oh dear and they said it again and again.

Oh dear they said oh dear.

And they found it very hard not to always say oh dear. They just always did say oh dear.

Oh dear.

Well there they were Nero and Nellie and Netty and Ned and they were all saying Oh dear.

It was all the fault of the alphabet being twenty-six letters with the half being thirteen.

So said Nero and Netty and Nellie and Ned, so if we have to have N which they say is what it is, and undoubtedly N is what it is well said Nero and Nellie and Netty and Ned since N is what it is let us just be as wicked as we can let us all be born on the thirteenth just to go with N that is Nero and Netty and Nellie and Ned and let us just never go to bed.

They all said yes let us never go to bed, let us never never go to bed. Let us be born all born on the thirteenth and let us never go to bed.

They decided and it was very wise of them to decide to do this because supposing they had said they would go to bed. Well supposing they had decided to go to bed, what would have happened, why they would have all been dead, that is what would have happened.

Oh dear, what would have happened, it was just that that would have happened. And so nothing happened because they did not go to bed.

Little by little each one of them got up instead of going to bed and they would begin to count and they would say perhaps there is a mistake, perhaps Monday is Sunday and perhaps thirteen is twelve, perhaps. And then one of them would slowly get up, you must remember they had none of them not one of the four of them not one of them had ever been in bed, and they would get up and they would say, perhaps they would say, oh dear, and then they would say, perhaps they counted wrong, perhaps Wednesday is Monday, perhaps it is and perhaps thirteen is twenty-five perhaps it is, and perhaps Saturday is Friday perhaps it is and perhaps N is X perhaps it is.

They just went on perhapsing like this until they almost fell asleep but they know they had said they would never go to bed and so what could they do they could get up but they could not go to bed and so this was what they did do. And so they went on Nero went on and Netty went on and Nellie went on and Ned was along and they all made a song.

If Friday was Monday

And Tuesday was Sunday

If Wednesday was Friday

And Saturday was Monday

If Sunday was Tuesday

And Wednesday was Friday

Who would say which was a lucky day and who could say whether there were more than there were yesterday or less than there were Friday.

Who said they, who knows when we were born.

Who knows.

And the cuckoo clock answered.

Who knows.

Who knows.

So said Nero they said clocks talk, they tell time, if we smash all the clocks nobody will know when we were born and we can say we were not born on any day they say. Yes let's, they all said, and they each of them got themselves a hammer and they began to smash clocks, and then some one saw them and said what are you doing. We are smashing clocks said Nero Netty Nellie and Ned, but why was said what have the clocks done, they have said we were born and we were not born we never go to bed we are not dead, and the clocks are always talking and they are always adding and we are tired of listening.

You can see what an awful letter N is, just an awful letter, and then all of a sudden a little clock began, it did not tell the time it made a chime and Nero and Nellie and Netty stopped hammering clocks and they stopped to listen and the little clock said go to bed go to bed, and Nero was sleepy and Nellie was sleepy and Netty was sleepy and Ned was sleepy, and as the little clock kept saying go to bed go to bed, well they did they just did go to bed, and each of them had a little bread and they laid their head on the pillow of the bed and they were not dead and they were asleep and all their troubles were over and they forgot to say oh dear, they said instead how nice it is to be here and that was all there was to it and they forgot the alphabet and they forgot thirteen and they forgot they were born and they were sweetly sleeping thinking they were eating strawberries in the dawn on the lawn.

And that is the end of the sad story of N which is not as sad as the story of M which is much sadder and badder, of course it is.

And now there is O.

O of course could not be sad O could only be glad.

Orlando Olga Only and Owen.

Believe it or not they really had these names. O always makes people like that.

My gracious said Orlando isn't it lovely the wind in the trees.

You mean the green trees said Olga, oh yes said Only the wind in the green trees. You mean said Owen the blue sky and the wind in the green trees. Oh yes said Orlando my gracious isn't it lovely.

Much as they were used to it they could not settle down to sit they had to run to meet some one.

That one said gracious me and Orlando said I said gracious me, and that one said well what makes you think you said gracious me.

Orlando stopped and said I don't know. I did say gracious me. He looked around at Olga and Only and Owen and they looked at him as if they did not know him.

What said Orlando did I not say gracious me. And nobody said anything.

Orlando was puzzled, had he said gracious me, had he said gracious me it is lovely or had he not.

Well anyway it was lovely, the wind in the trees was lovely, the green trees and the blue sky but had he said the trees were green and the sky was blue, had he.

He stood and looked and Olga and Only and Owen looked as if they did not see him.

Orlando began to feel very funny.

Suppose said Orlando I get them away from here will they then look at me as if they did not see me. I wonder.

And slowly Orlando went away and neither Olga nor Only nor Owen followed after.

Pretty soon Owen saw another tree and he said gracious me the wind in the tree is lovely.

And he looked around and he found that Olga was there and she said the green in the tree and Orlando said yes the green in the tree gracious me isn't it lovely and he looked again and there was Only looking at him as if he had seen him, and Orlando said yes the wind in the green tree gracious me isn't it lovely and Only said yes and the blue sky and Orlando said yes gracious me oh my the wind in the green tree against the blue sky isn't it lovely.

And Orlando looked around but Owen was not anywhere around and he said dear me gracious me oh my I could cry everything feels so funny.

So Orlando went away and he had nothing to say and Olga and Only came after and they went away and they could not see that Owen was there too until suddenly they heard a hullabaloo and there was Owen up in the tree and they could not try to say good-bye because Owen made such a noise there was no reason why that they should try.

So all of a sudden Orlando said I have had enough you all go away, I am going alone, you can go home if you have a home, Orlando began to be

very bitter if you have a home, I said Orlando said I am going to try to see if I can see the man who said I did not say gracious me.

So Orlando started off but the others came after, because Orlando was right, they had no home so they had to roam and why not follow Orlando. If you have no home you have to follow and you try to say hulloa but really it is better to follow.

So they started off but Orlando was cross and he would not know they were there.

Well were they there. Olga and Only and Owen.

Orlando said they were not there, they said they were there, well anyway what did they care they none of them had any home to go to.

So they started to see if everywhere the wind was in the trees the trees were green and the sky was blue, and gradually they knew that it was true that everywhere the wind was in the trees the trees were green and the sky was blue, that is nothing new but it is true and they wandered on for they had no home and what is the use of making a moan if you have no home and it is true that the wind is in the trees and the trees are green and the sky is blue.

As yet there was nothing else to do and they had no home.

So Orlando said he had rather be alone, but they said no no they would not go, they would go with him. They had not meant not to see him when that other one had said that he Orlando had not said gracious me the wind in the tree. No said the three they had not meant anything they would follow Orlando. What else could they do, they had no home, no indeed no home, no home.

It is funny not to have a home very funny but it does happen to a great many. When you say funny sometimes it makes you laugh and sometimes when you say funny oh my it makes you cry.

That is what happened to Orlando and Olga and Only and Owen, they said it was funny not to have a home but when they said funny oh my it made them cry.

So they began to wonder why, why they had no home and they knew it was true they had no home. But they had a birthday each one of them had a birthday and if they each one of them had a birthday well then they must have been born and if they had been born they must have had a home everybody can say that there has to be a home to have a birthday and now oh dear where had it gone away, not the birthday they each still had one, but the home. The home the home.

So then they began, they could not remember back had they all had the same home, had Orlando had the same as Olga, had Only had the same as Owen, they could not remember but they did not think so and why because as much as they could try they could not remember always having been together. And when they were like this they never thought to give each other a kiss they just thought they would not look as if they knew who was who.

And slowly Orlando grew stout, that made it difficult for him to move about.

And then Olga slowly grew thin, that made it difficult for her to win any one to come to lunch, she had nothing to eat and so it was not a treat for her to want any one to come to lunch.

And slowly Only grew long and that was a bother because beds are short and he was long, he could not stretch out, he had to put a chair there beside his bed to either put his feet on or his head. It was not much fun being too long, he never thought it was funny very long.

And slowly Owen was short, short and shorter until anybody thought he could be bought, kept to show in a circus or what, well that was not a way he liked to be bought, and so every day and in every way he got a little shorter and if so and they bought him to show well in a little while he would go because he would be too short to see, and that would not be at all funny.

So there they were, no home, no nothing but each one of them had a birthday, and pretty soon each one knew that rather than anything they would like a room, it might just as well be a moon but a moon was always changing its shape and a room well a room ought to be always there with a window and a door and a ceiling and a floor. Finally they knew Orlando and Olga and Only and Owen that it was the O that made them go so funny.

So then they said if they could only get rid of the O and so they tried that way but only Owen could say his name without the O, he might be called Wen but then if he were called Wen where was his birthday, his birthday was for Owen. The others just could not say their names without the O, just try it and you will see that is so, so having no home they just each one of them was on the go all night and all day, which any one can say is not a pleasant way.

So then they thought they would collect stamps. They had to do something so they just thought they would collect stamps and if they collected enough stamps they might find one that would lead them home.

This was not much of a success. Orlando liked to lick stamps but he did not like to keep them, Olga hated stamps, Only liked stamps but he could not read and Owen he was always the best of the four and sometimes he thought if he only was not with them somebody would take him to a home and he would not have to roam.

Well that did happen to Owen, somebody said little as he was they would take him they liked him little only he would have to have a new birthday and begin again well would he. He thought and thought and all he could say was well would he.

Well would he.

This is all there is about it, well would he.

And then there was Orlando, he was so stout he could not get about and so he stayed where he was and if you stay where you are long enough then that place gets to be your home. Well that was all right for Orlando only he was so large he did not have birthday enough to go around, so he thought he might as well go and get drowned. But if you are very stout you cannot drown, so what could he do, he had to have a birthday and he was so stout that his birthday could not get all about him. Oh dear what could he do. What could he.

Well what could he.

And then there was Olga she was so thin that she had not place enough to win being her home, she was thin she could not fit in and so it could not be her home, so she said she would she would stay, but did she, if she did her birthday would be a bother to her because birthdays have to be able to see the one whose birthday they are and Olga was so thin the birthday could not see her, so would she get out to try to be stout and keep her birthday, now would she.

Now would she.

And now there was Only and Only was so long, all along Only was so long he was so long all along that he was all along because he was so long.

So how could he have a home and a birthday, would the birthday be in his head or in his feet, and would either his head or his feet be a treat for his poor birthday. His poor birthday said every birthday oh dear.

And so Only would only hear oh dear, and his feet would only hear oh dear, so what did Only do.

Now what did Only do.

What did Only do.

So you see this is the end of O's and who knows when you say it is funny it will make you laugh or cry, oh my.

And now there is P.

P is really funny.

Peter Paul Pearl and Pancake.

Peter's birthday was the first of January.

Paul's birthday was the second of February.

Pearl's birthday was the third of March and Pancake's birthday was the fourth of July.

It just did happen that way they did not try but it just did happen that way.

Peter was an old man, he had a daughter and she had five children. Peter lived far away and so on the first of January all five children had to write him on his birthday. They did not say but they felt that way why did he have to have a birthday and they did not say but they felt that way and they did say why did he have to have a birthday the first of January. It was not very convenient naturally, in the first place there was Christmas and he was far away and it was almost Christmas Day and they all five had to write to him on his birthday. They had not yet their Christmas gifts so what could they say, what could anybody say to a grandfather far away on his birthday the first of January when they had not yet had Christmas candy. Oh dear. It was queer but there it was, it had to be done, and before the setting sun, the sun was setting and not any one of the five of them had even begun the letter to their grandfather on his birthday. Well there they were all five of them and each one had to write a different one, and they had such lovely paper their mother had given to them, and they had such lovely ink and such lovely pens and never a thing to say to grandfather so very far away. To be sure they had never seen him but they knew his name was Peter and their mother she said he was sweeter than any one and he sent them nice presents when they came but dear me they had not come.

So there they sat and they were not allowed to chat and their mother came in to see them begin. Not one of them had begun, not one, they had said dear grandpapa, each one had said dear grandpapa and then they were done.

So the oldest said mother darling mother, give me the first sentence the first sentence is such a bother, and then with that one I can go on like anything. So the mother said all right, I will show you how to begin. And me and me, cried each one, so she gave each one a beginning and then she went away singing.

It did seem so easy to write what she had told them and they stopped, how could they go on, well just how could they go on. Tomorrow was coming and the sun was setting and if they had thought of anything they would certainly be forgetting but they had not thought of anything to forget no not yet.

And so they sat and they looked at the cat and the cat went out into the setting sun and oh dear me their letters were only just begun.

So their mother came in again to see how they were getting on. Oh dear dear mother they all said, our pens are as heavy as lead, what do we say next, we have all begun, see how we have all begun but what do we say next. Well what did they say next, she had to tell each one something they said next and then she said now only work and you will be done and she went away into the setting sun.

Oh dear the sun was setting more and more, you could see it on the floor and not one of them could think of anything more oh dear oh dear oh dear if only there was an open door. But there was none. Well there they were and it was almost night and their mother came in to see if they were all right. Well they were all right, if you call it all right to know you would have to stay there all night to make the letter go right. Not one of them had written anything, they just could not think of anything to say to their grandfather far away and on his birthday.

So it seemed it was almost the next day but really it was only a little while when their mother was back to see what a pile they had been writing. Well there it was, it was just as it was, each letter was just as it was and all five of them were sitting. Oh mother dear they said it is very clear that if you would only tell us how to end then it would be a wonderful letter we would send, oh mother dear do tell us how to end. So the mother told each one what to say to make it done and they did and that was that and they felt they felt they could get a hat and go out in the clear night and have a pleasant fright and how they had done everything in the way that was right and with all their might.

The moral of this story is the grandfathers who are far away should not have their birthdays on the first of January, they had much better choose another day for their birthday.

P. Peter Paul Pearl and Pancake.

Paul was not a grandfather, he was a grandchild and he was wild he was so spoiled and he just thought every day was his birthday just any and every day because he was spoiled that way.

He thought everything was a theatre performing just for him, his grandmother his mother and his father and he could mimic every one, he could make believe he was chauffeur waiting for his mother, he could make believe he was a girl who had robbed her brother, he could make believe he was his own grandfather, he could make believe he was a beggar, he could make believe he was a boy who had lost his mother, he could make believe he had been run over, he could make believe he was frightened and would change his home for another, he could make believe that he had a sister and that he had lost her and had found another, he could make believe anything and his father said he would send him away to school but he was so spoiled the school would not keep him so he was home again making believe everything.

One day he made believe that fourteen was twelve. He made believe it was, then he made believe that five was three, he made believe it was, then he made believe his home was burned down he made believe it was and then he made believe that a girl he knew had forty dogs. When he made believe this girl he knew had forty dogs he made believe that all forty followed him, they followed him all forty of them and they ate everything all forty of them and they bit every one all forty of them and Paul made believe they would go on biting every one and eating every one until there would be nothing or not anything left alive any more anywhere. While Paul was making believe this thing he made believe that the forty dogs would always do whatever he told them and he made believe he was telling them to kill everybody and everything and then he made believe that he would make the forty dogs kill each other and bite and eat them and then he Paul could make believe that he was the only one living and that everyday was his birthday.

But while he was making believe this thing the forty dogs turned on him, they bit him and he ran away, he did not make believe running away he just ran and ran and ran away and that was the end of him.

Pearl was not like him at all, Pearl was a girl.

When she knew who was who, she was astonished too.

It astonished her to know she was a girl.

Who are you they asked her and she said she was Pearl.

And what is pearl they said to her, and she said Pearl is a girl.

Every time she said Pearl is a girl she was astonished.

That is the kind of a girl Pearl was.

She was the kind that is astonished.

She was astonished by everything.

She was astonished when she went in bathing.

Water astonished her, everything astonished her and what astonished her most was everything. She was like that.

So then she decided to go on being astonished. And so the first thing that happened to her she decided was very astonishing. And what was that first thing that was happening. Well the first thing that happened to her was to be born and that certainly was very astonishing.

She just was astonished. There she was, she was born and her name was Pearl and Pearl was a girl and it was all very astonishing. It certainly was.

Then the next thing that happened to her was to have a birthday and that was certainly an astonishing thing to say, Pearl was a girl and she had a birthday. She was so astonished she just stopped everything but everything astonished Pearl that was the kind of a girl Pearl was.

You would suppose that she would get used to being Pearl and to Pearl's being a girl but not at all it rolled along like a ball this being astonished by everything.

Supposing she got up in the morning, well she found the morning astonishing and when she went to bed at night well you might say she was not very bright but she did find the bed and the night very astonishing.

She found her head astonishing and her feet and her hands and her hair. She did not care, she just would say what she thought and she did think it was astonishing she thought it was all astonishing. That was the kind of a girl Pearl was Pearl was that kind of a girl she found everything astonishing.

And then she met Pancake, that was his name Mr. Pancake. Now you might have supposed that she would find that astonishing that his name was Mr. Pancake and that she met him but not at all, she did not find him astonishing at all, she just ate him and after that, well after that, well it made her feel funny to have eaten him and after that well after that nothing was astonishing, that was the kind of a girl Pearl was, she was that kind of a girl.

Q is for Quiet, Queenie, Quintet and Question.

It is hard to have names like that. Very very hard, it makes anybody troubled to have names like that, very very troubled but all the same they had them.

Mr. and Mrs. Quiet
Miss Queenie
Mr. Quintet
and Master Question.

The night was all around them and they were wondering if it was thundering and very likely it was.

That is the way Mr. and Mrs. Quiet were, they were always wondering whether it was. They had no rabbits no hens, they had goats no boats, they had sheep no lambs and they had no cows, they had leaves no grass and they had bread no cake and they were always awake. That was the kind of husband and wife Mr. and Mrs. Quiet were. They had tongues and no teeth, they had knives and no forks, they had spoons and no bread, they had no hair on their head, that is the kind of a couple Mr. and Mrs. Quiet were.

Once in a while they had potatoes, once in a while they had cabbage, once in a while they had wood to chew and once in a while they drank water. Once in a while. They led a very happy life Mr. and Mrs. Quiet.

They had a bicycle but they did not ride it they pushed it and on it they put their cabbages when they had them and their potatoes when they had them and behind them went their goats and at home were their rabbits and they were very comfortable every day that is what they did say Mr. and Mrs. Quiet.

They had a favorite rabbit Mr. and Mrs. Quiet and he was the only rabbit they had who had a birthday. He was a very big rabbit a very bad rabbit and he had the habit of always eating a little rabbit on his birthday, a very very bad habit, but Mr. and Mrs. Quiet could never quiet that habit it was the habit of this rabbit. And they thought, one day they thought that if they made believe that he was caught and that they would tell him what they thought of this habit of eating a baby rabbit on his birthday that it would cure him, but it did not, on his next birthday he went back to his habit of eating a baby rabbit.

So they thought Mr. and Mrs. Quiet thought of taking away his birthday and in that way he would be cured of the habit of eating a little rabbit on his birthday.

Well what happened.

Nothing and then it was a terrible thing, they took away his birthday and so he did not know what day was his birthday so just to be sure he ate a little rabbit every day just as if every day was his birthday. He was a ferocious rabbit and Mr. and Mrs. Quiet did not know what to say, there he was eating a little rabbit every day.

Mr. and Mrs. Quiet did not know what to say if they let the rabbit run away, well they tried that but he wanted to stay he just would not run away and they could not kill him and eat him because after all he was their favorite rabbit. Then they decided to get the best of him, they gave away every rabbit they had, just gave them away and then when it was the big rabbit's birthday he looked around for a little rabbit to eat on that day, and there were no little rabbits they

all had been given away. So he refused to eat anything, he was mad and he refused cabbages and carrots and everything, he would not eat anything he was just mad. And Mr. and Mrs. Quiet did not know whether to be sad or glad and then they decided to be glad. The next day the big rabbit refused to eat anything, it was not his birthday but he refused anything even on an ordinary day because he had not had a little rabbit for his birthday. So there were Mr. and Mrs. Quiet looking at the big rabbit and the big rabbit looking at them and the eyes of Mr. and Mrs. Quiet were full of tears they were worried like anything about the big rabbit and the big rabbit's eyes grew redder and redder he had begun by having pink eyes but he had eaten so many little rabbits on his birthday that his eyes grew redder and redder and then an awful thing was happening, the big rabbit's eyes grew redder and redder and Mr. and Mrs. Quiet who were looking at him found him more and more alarming and then all of a sudden the big rabbit's red eyes burst out into flame, the big rabbit was on fire inside him and he and the cabbages and carrots he had not eaten were all flaming and the smoke and fire were coming out of him and the little house he lived in was burning and Mr. and Mrs. Quiet who were looking at him found it all terrifying, they were so frightened they could not do anything, they could not get any water to put the fire out they were so frightened they could not move about and so they just sat there watching and pretty soon it was over the burning there was nothing left of the big rabbit but a red cinder and that Mr. and Mrs. Quiet put out by dropping tears on him. And after that Mr. and Mrs. Quiet lived very quietly with their goats and everything but they never after had another rabbit.

Miss Queenie and Master Question and Mr. Quintet never had anything like that happen to them. They never had cared not any of them for goats or rabbits or anything. What they liked was fish in the morning, beef at noon and eggs in the evening. That is all they cared about. Miss Queenie said it made her stout to eat trout, Master Question said that beef gave him indigestion and Mr. Quintet said he always when he saw an egg he Mr. Quintet always said not yet. And still what was there to do, there was fish in the morning, beef at noon and eggs in the evening and the more often it was happening the more often Miss Queenie said trout in the morning made her stout and Master Question said beef at noon gave him Master Question indigestion and Mr. Quintet said whenever he saw an egg he Mr. Quintet said Not yet.

And so they thought they ought to think of something so they thought and they thought that they ought each one of them to think of something. So then they thought that if each one brought something they would not have fish in the morning beef at noon and eggs in the evening. But what could they bring, anybody could ring but what could they bring.

So they said we could give each other something. Now we do not know said they when it is each other's birthday, so let us play that any day is one of each other's birthday and then we could bring something for that day. Yes they would say but then say today which one of us will get what we bring and which two of us will bring, on a birthday others bring but the one who has the birthday he gets everything, well now how, how can we know which will bring and which will get everything.

Naturally a thing like that would mean quarreling. Miss Queenie, she being a girl and she knew she was a pretty girl at least she said she knew she was a pretty girl because she had a curl, well anyway she said they should do the bringing and she would do the receiving, but not at all said Master Question, that is out of the question, to be sure you are a girl and you may have a curl perhaps yes perhaps no it is only you who tell us so, but I I who am always in question, I who have indigestion, I will receive everything to decide what part I will keep and what I will divide, and beside said Master Question it is my right to have a birthday because I am so bright every day.

Then Mr. Quintet said Not yet Not yet, Mr. Quintet always said Not yet, he said Not yet, he said do not let no he said do not let any one think that it is not for me to decide about how to divide everything. I am Mr. Quintet, that means there are five of me yet and so you bet I will not let any one divide anything.

Well there they were they could not decide not about birthdays or anything so they just went on, and there was fish in the morning and beef at noon and eggs at night, and Miss Queenie said trout in the morning made her stout and Master Question said beef at noon gave him Master Question indigestion, and Mr. Quintet said eggs at night, when I see them all right I always say I Mr. Quintet I always say Not yet.

So they all three live on very unhappily and they never decided anything about their birthday.

You have to say the whole alphabet almost to get to *R* because Q always throws you out. Now everybody knows that. So there is R, R rolls around and around like a ball not that it is a ball not at all. **R** for Robert, Redbreast, Rachel and Rosy.

Rose had a dog a little dog named Chilly.

Chilly was his name and chilly was his nature.

That is in winter, in summer it was another matter.

In the summer he was as mad as could be.

Rosy said to him remember Chilly how cold you were in the winter.

But Chilly said no it is summer and I will kill everything, you see you just watch me.

And Rosy did she just watched Chilly and she saw that one thing led to another and then to one thing more.

Chilly began by barking at his dinner. He barked very hard at his dinner. Then he ate his dinner. Then Chilly began of course this was summer he began to be warmer and warmer and one thing followed after another. He saw a chicken and he thought a chicken with its feathers on must be hot, so he went after it like a shot, and it was too big to kill, not that really Chilly would want to kill it, but he did want it to be still so he could take all its feathers off until there would be no feathers on it, and it would be nice and cool and perhaps would go swimming in a pool.

Rosy tried to save it but Chilly wanted to shave it shave all its feathers off by pulling them out of course, and so he did and Rosy was cross because everybody would say that they would take Chilly away and everybody would be cross of course, cross with Rosy because Chilly was such a little silly, it was Rosy's fault of course.

And so Rosy tried to take Chilly away from the chicken where it lay and then Chilly decided to play it was a mouse's birthday. He did play that it was a mouse's birthday, five little mousies were born and Chilly said there would not be any harm in running after the mother mouse now that the little mousies were born, so he chased the mother mouse away and later in the day he found her again and what shall I say, well Chilly made away with the mother mouse that day, the day the little mousies were born and even though it was warm the little mousies born that day never had another birthday.

And this was a day of Rosy's little dog Chilly whom everybody said was silly but he was not at all silly, and in the summer he was not chilly, no it was Rosy who was silly to let Chilly do whatever he wanted to. But they just went on every day, Rosy and Chilly and in the summer when it was warm Chilly did a lot of harm, not really very much harm because he was so little and that is what Rosy always said, she said let him alone in the winter he is so chilly let him do what he likes when he is warm, and so they did and so Chilly did, and Chillys do and so do Rosys and in the winter they sit by the fire and wink and think of what they did in the summer and what they will do another summer and so there they are and is it fair to mousies and chickens that they sit there by the fire and stare Chilly and Rosy, but perhaps yes and perhaps no, well believe it or not it is true that is what Chillys and Rosys and chickens and mousies will do.

Robert was a boy well he was grown up now and yet he was not bigger than he had been, when he said when had I been, and they said do not tell him but call him Bobolink and that will make him think that he is bigger yet. Not yet said Bobolink.

When they called him Bobolink it made him think of Miss Robin-Red-Breast.

Bobolink had a mother and she said Robert, when I call you Bobolink what do you love best.

Robert went pink he said when you call me Bobolink I love Miss Robin-Red-Breast best.

So Bobolink tried to get married beside, to get married to Miss Robin-Red-Breast, his bride, but he couldn't and why, it will make you cry, he couldn't because he caught measles.

Imagine that, his mother was there and she said take care, if you think of Miss Robin-Red-Breast all day perhaps you will get that way, spotted red and right there ahead of Robert called Bobolink was measles and measles is red oh dear said Bobolink if my hair had been red, my measles could not spread, oh dear said poor Bobolink.

But he had measles and he had to stay in bed all day and he had to stay awake all night and everybody gave him something all day, well that was perhaps like a birthday. Sometimes measles does take you that way.

So he went on having measles every day and so he could not get married that day, of course nobody ever got married having measles nobody, and then it was the fourteenth of February, it was Saint Valentine's day and surely said Bobolink surely those naughty measles will go away.

But they didn't, they looked as if they were going to stay they acted as if they were going to stay they talked as if they were going to stay and it was no use for poor Bobolink to tell them about Saint Valentine's day and how he was to be married even if he had to be carried to dear Miss Robin-Red-Breast that day.

But it was no use he could not get married he had measles red spotted measles and he could not get married that day.

So Valentine's Day was yesterday and they were not married that day and perhaps Miss Robin-Red-Breast would fly away if they could not get married soon some way, might fly far far far away.

So what could poor Bobolink do, it was true what could poor Bobolink do, the measles looked as if they had come to stay and Miss Robin-Red-Breast might fly far far far away if they did not get married some way.

So Bobolink thought and thought and then he thought perhaps measles have a birthday, if they have a birthday then they would have to go away that day to celebrate their birthday, sure enough they would have to go away for that day.

But how could Bobolink make the measles say they had a birthday and on what day.

Bobolink thought and thought but he could think of no way. Of course if he asked the measles if they had a birthday of course they would say what is a birthday, we never heard of a birthday, naturally measles never did pay any attention to anybody's birthday, it was their way.

And then Bobolink thought and he said I will ask not all measles but just one little red one little red spot that little red spot could not know what is what just that one little red spot, I'll find it all alone and I'll make a moan and ask it to tell and perhaps if I ask it very well the little red spot which looks like a dot, I'll tell it what will I tell I'll tell it that if it does not tell it will get shot.

Well he did ask Bobolink did ask the little red spot, the little red measle spot when measles have a birthday, and he said if the little red spot would not not tell when the measles had their birthday, well that little red spot would get shot. So it did tell, it could not very well not tell, and it told that the measles' birthday was the very next day.

So then Bobolink knew that just that day all the measles would be away celebrating their birthday and so quickly he sent his mother to tell Miss Robin-Red-Breast to get dressed and come the next day, and they were married that day and they lived happily ever after and they never ever saw any measles again.

Rachel was another story, she just lived for glory, she said I was born to glory, and they said what is glory and she said look at me and they did and what did they see they thought they saw Rachel but did they. They did not, what, no they did not, because Rachel was not there, she was gone to glory, so they said, where is she gone and she said with scorn do you not know where I am gone I am gone to glory. This is the story. Rachel was born that did her no harm, she had a birthday that did not take her away, she had another birthday and she found a thorn and the thorn said it was born that day, and Rachel did say no nobody was born today, I was born today and nobody else has today for their birthday. The thorn was torn when Rachel threw it away and the thorn did say it is my birthday and Rachel did say the glory of this day is that it is my birthday. This led to everything and Rachel was no more and the thorn was on the floor and Rachel was gone, she was gone to glory and that is all there is to her story.

Now it is easy to remember that S comes after R, very easy to remember very very easy to remember very very very easy to remember that S comes after R. Nobody would think that R comes after S that would be a mess, so S comes after R but they stick close together like tar, they are filled with tenderness oh yes, R and S.

Really my wife says S. For all my life says R. Really begins with R and S begins S, yes yes.

And T comes after S and can anybody guess oh yes oh yes oh yes how completely yes T comes after S. Believe it or not it is true if not new, true.

And now for S.

Sammy and Sally and Save and Susy.

Sammy had his aunt and his aunt had Sammy and his aunt's name was Fanny and Fanny had Sammy.

Sammy was his name and he was funny and he had an aunt Fanny and she was funny.

Sammy could not eat bread or potatoes or chocolate or cake or eggs or butter or even a date, if he did he fainted away, that was his way, a very funny way but it was Sammy's way. His aunt Fanny was not funny that way, but she

was funny in another way, whenever she saw a cat or dog a turtle or a bird or a third, a third of anything she had to turn away. She was funny that way.

But Sammy had his aunt Fanny and Aunt Fanny had her Sammy.

Poor dear Sammy.

Now what could he eat, what could be a treat, poor dear Sammy.

A lemonade perhaps or a beefsteak, or a plate or a but dear me no not ice cream, he could not eat cream, nor a birthday cake, he could eat the candles but not the cake, poor dear Sammy.

Sample and example.

His Aunt Fanny did not care that Sammy could not share what she ate, she just went on cooking and eating and Sammy just went on looking and fainting. They were very funny Sammy and his Aunt Fanny. Poor dear Sammy.

And in spite of all Sammy grew tall tall enough to go to school.

In school they were taught

Sample and Example.

There was a pretty girl and she had a curl and her name was Sally. They called her pretty Sally and she was a sample. And then there was Sammy there just was Sammy poor dear Sammy and he was an example.

And then one day pretty Sally in play asked Sammy to come to her house on her birthday.

Sammy did.

There was a great big cake with frosting and a date and Sammy feeling faint said he could not eat icing or the date or cake but he could eat candles if they were to be given. But no said Sally oh no don't you know, we burn them, there are no candles when we come to eating we burn them and if we did not burn them I would not have my next one not my next birthday, oh naughty Sammy wants to take my next birthday away.

And poor Sammy had nothing to say, to see all that icing and cake made him feel faint so he just did have to go away.

Now you may think this is a funny story but no it is true, anybody even you could know Sammy poor dear Sammy and his Aunt Fanny, he lives there too and it is true all the story of Sammy all the story of his Aunt Fanny all the story of Aunt Fanny all the story of Sammy is true. Poor dear Sammy.

Save and Susie were twins.

And when that begins

They just go on being twins.

Saturday is an awful day they used to say but you would not expect that twins would object to Saturday.

But they did.

They just did object to Saturday.

Now what could be a reason for this.

Saturday ought to be full of bliss.

But there is nothing to say they did object to Saturday.

And the reason for it was this.

Twins can have cousins of course,

And cousins can make twins cross,

And these twins they had cousins,

And you could never guess

But the cousins of these twins,

Were triplets, no less.

And they did come every Saturday

To stay all day with the twins,

And that made the twins very cross,

Because instead of two and two being four and no more,

It was two and three which was very nasty,

Because it was it all ways was three and two and nobody could like that not they or you not at all. And so it was two and three which makes five and that was not all.

The triplets had cousins too and what do you think these cousins were they quadruplets much more yet than triplets or twins, oh so much more and when it begins oh so much more, and these quadruplets came to play every Saturday with the triplets and twins and every Saturday was a worse day so you see why the twins were cross of course.

And then what did the quadruplets have they had cousins too and these cousins were quintuplets, just think of that and they came every Saturday to play so it made the twins just two, and the triplets just three, and the quadruplets four and no more and the quintuplets five and every one of them alive.

It was more than the twins could endure and they hated Saturday more and more, and they used to roll on the floor to say how they hated Saturday more and more.

And this was not all.

The twins had their birthday on the same day being twins that was of course and that did not make them cross, but when they had their birthday the triplets and the quadruplets and the quintuplets came to stay and eat all the birthday cake away, why not, when they were only twins and the others were triplets and quadruplets and quintuplets what could twins do against that, they might just as well have been one cat,

Oh dear.

And then the triplets had their birthday of course all three on the same day and the twins went there but naturally they did not care to because they were only twins and there were the triplets well the triplets did not care for it either, they were better than twins they were three against two it was true when it came to eat their birthday cake but what were three when the quadruplets and quintuplets were there who did not care about triplets and twins not at all.

And then the quadruplets had their birthday they of course were all four born on the same day and the twins and the triplets came too to say how do you do but the four and the quintuplets were there well naturally triplets and twins did not get their share.

And the quintuplets had their birthday and that was more still because there were five all born the same day and all eating their cake away, the quadruplets and the triplets and the twins naturally had no share, the quintuplets were there.

So you can see what the twins felt about Saturday, it was all right to be twins but other things Save and Susie said it was too much they hated it to be such, such a way to be, to be nothing but twins and have cousins who were triplets whose cousins were quadruplets whose cousins were quintuplets, it certainly was too much, and Save and Susie the twins rolled on the floor to say they would not stand it any more.

But there was nothing to do every Saturday was there and every birthday too and there was nothing to do for the twins but to boohoo which they did every day before and after when they would all get together and they were only twins only only twins each one only a twin and so they never could win when there were cousins of triplets, quadruplets and quintuplets, no no no, it is even so.

The moral of which is do not only be twins but if you are twins do not have cousins and if you have cousins do not have them be triplets and quadruplets and quintuplets. No no no, it should not be arranged so, but Save and Susie could not change, if you are twins and that begins you just go on being twins.

And now there is T.

Thornie and Tillie and Tender and True.

And after T well there are a lot of useless letters, just think of them all U V W X Y Z, just think of them all there they are pushed up at the end just like a ball, and there is nothing to do at all not with them all but just the same they each have a name so useless they are but they cannot be put into a jar and they cannot be covered with tar they must be just made to go just as if it was not so that there was no use in their being there just to stare.

But first comes T and that is like you or me a very necessary T.

Thornie and Tillie and Tender and True.

Thornie Rose and Tillie Brown had never lived in a town.

Thornie's mother was a missionary in China.

Tillie's father was a missionary in China.

Thornie swam in the river with little Chinese boys.

Tillie sang songs with little Chinese girls.

And then one day Tillie saw Thornie and Thornie saw Tillie.

There were so many little Chinese boys and little Chinese girls around that you could hardly see the ground but Thornie saw Tillie and Tillie saw Thornie, and they were both there.

So Thornie said he would not swim he said he would talk to Tillie and all the Chinese boys said that was silly, but all the same Tillie and Thornie began and Tillie was to sing but when she saw Thornie she did not sing, she did not even begin but she said she would talk to Thornie and the little Chinese girls all said to Tillie but that is silly, but Thornie and Tillie did not think it was silly and that is what they did say. Thornie and Tilly.

Thornie Rose and his mother Mrs. Rose and Tillie Brown and her father Mr. Brown were standing and around them were miles and miles of them Chinamen and Chinese women and Chinese children, miles and miles and miles of them and they were all singing.

Tender and true and all for you.

And as they were singing Tender and True and all for you there were more and more of them Chinese men and Chinese women and Chinese children and there were more and more miles of them more miles of Chinese men and Chinese women and Chinese children they were singing Tender and True and all for you and then Thornie Rose and Mrs. Rose and Tillie Brown and Mr. Brown began singing too, Tender and True and all for you and all of them the miles and miles and more miles and miles of Chinese men and Chinese women and Chinese children and Thornie Rose and Mrs. Rose and Tillie Brown and Mr. Brown were singing Tender and True and all for you and they went on singing all of them went on singing and then it was morning and they all went on singing, singing and singing Tender and True and all for you and then it was evening.

And then they decided to go to bed but how could they go to bed when there were not any beds to go to bed in and so as there were no beds to go to bed in they went on singing Tender and True and all for you.

And then everybody sat down all the miles and miles and more miles and miles of Chinese men and Chinese women and Chinese children and Thornie Rose and Mrs. Rose and Tillie Brown and Mr. Brown. And when they were all sat down they all began to frown.

Then they all said this will not do it will not do for us all to sit down and frown no it will not do, so they all said all the miles and miles and more and more miles of Chinese men and Chinese women and Chinese children and Thornie Rose and Mrs. Rose and Tillie Brown and Mr. Brown, they all said what shall we do since it will not do to just sit down and frown.

So they decided that each one should tell something, they should tell about the day they were born, but said the miles and miles and more and more miles of Chinese men and Chinese women and Chinese children and Thornie Rose and Mrs. Rose and Tillie Brown and Mr. Brown we do not remember when we were born.

And they all once more began to sit down and frown.

This will never do we must do something they all said we might just as well be dead if we were never born.

Of course we were born said all the miles and miles of Chinamen and Chinese women and Chinese children and more and more miles of them and Thornie Rose and Mrs. Rose and Tillie Brown and Mr. Brown, of course we were born. Well perhaps if we keep on remembering we can remember being born. Well they went on remembering all of them but they could not remember the day they were born they remembered the first birthday but they could not remember the day they were born and then the miles and miles of Chinamen and Chinese women and Chinese children and the more and more miles of them and Thornie Rose and Mrs. Rose and Tillie Brown and Mr. Brown they wondered if it would do them any harm if they could not remember the day they were born.

They all had something to say about the day they were born and every birthday they had had since the day they were born and they went on to say everything they had to say each one of them was saying everything they had to say about the day they were born and every birthday they had had since that day and as they were all telling it all of them the miles and miles of Chinese men and Chinese women and Chinese children and the more and more miles of Chinese men and Chinese women and Chinese children and Thornie Rose and Mrs. Rose and Tillie Brown and Mr. Brown the night passed away and they all had forgotten to frown and so then it was the next day and as soon as it was the next day they all began to sing Tender and True and all for you, and so everything was gay and everybody had had something to say and now everybody had something to sing Tender and True and all for you and that was the end of everything, and they all lived happily along and they never forgot their song Tender and True and all for you not any of them not the miles and miles of Chinamen and Chinese women and Chinese children and more and more and more miles of Chinese men and Chinese women and Chinese children and Thornie Rose and Mrs. Rose and Tillie Brown and Mr. Brown.

This all sounds funny but give them money and it is not funny.

Oh yes oh no of course.

This is of course

If no one is ever cross,

Of course of course.

And then you can sing Tender and True and all for you and this is that thing.

The end of the beginning.

The beginning of the ending.

Of course.

As I said T is the last letter that is not funny after that all the letters are as funny as money of course they are.

There is U.

U. Uno, Una, Ursula and United.

Uno and Una.

Uno knew Una and Una knew Uno.

You know that.

Uno was a boy and Una was a girl and Uno's eyes were blue and Una's eyes were brown, and Una's eyes were blue and Uno's eyes were brown. You know that.

Well perhaps it was not just like that. Uno was a boy. You know that, and Uno had one eye that was blue and one eye that was brown and this sounds as if it were not true but it is true you know that. And Una was a girl and she had two eyes too and one eye was blue and one of her eyes was brown. You know that, so Uno and Una one was a boy and one was a girl but each one had one blue eye and each one had one brown eye, and it sounds as if it were not true but it was true you know that.

Uno's right eye was blue and his left eye was brown and Una's left eye was blue and her right eye was brown.

Uno and Una they could both look up and down. But you know that.

What happened when each one had one eye which was brown and one eye which was blue. What did happen.

They were Uno and Una and what did happen.

Well you know what did happen.

Uno's mother had an eye which was blue and an eye which was brown but not Uno's father he had two eyes just the same there were two and they were both blue.

Una's father had an eye which was blue and an eye which was brown but not Una's mother. She had two eyes which were the same both eyes were brown.

But you can see that Uno having a mother with one eye brown and one eye blue and Una having a father like that too one eye brown and one eye blue, it was natural for Uno and for Una when they looked at each other to look with one eye brown and one eye blue and to see another with one eye brown and one eye blue too.

So there they were and naturally well it was natural enough they were married one to the other and they had quite a lot of little children and every single one of all of them had one eye brown and one eye blue.

Well that was the way they were born and of course it did make a great deal of a bother, not when they were all there together it was a rather nice mixture of brown and blue and when they looked at you it was kind of funny nobody exactly knew which was who and beside that if they opened one eye and closed one eye well how would you know whether their eyes were brown and blue. It was a good deal of a bother, not to a sister or to a brother because they were all alike and it just made them bright to have two eyes different one from the other but to any one else it was a good deal of a bother.

And then there was the question of clothes and birthdays. You always match the eyes in little girls' clothes and little boys' shirts and ties, and what could you do if one eye is brown and one eye is blue just what could one do, how could they match the color.

And then there was the birthday cake when each one had a birthday to celebrate, the candles on the birthday cake should match the color of the eyes everybody knows that is wise and what color could the candles be that lit the birthday cake of any of the three, just what color could it be, oh dear, it was a difficult thing to decide and then the one whose birthday cake it was and who had it to cut if he shut the brown eye the brown candles looked shy and if he shut the blue eye the blue candles would try to look away. It was not a natural thing to have two colors of candles and icing on a birthday cake but oh my however you try what could you do if you wanted to match the color of the eye.

Because you know however you try when you cut a birthday cake you always shut one eye. Oh my it was a bother and they could never decide what to do brown or blue.

And then one day there was a war and papa Uno went away to the war. You know he went away. And when he was away oh dear they shot one eye away, it was the blue eye and they made a glass eye and when he came back from the war he did not any more have one brown eye and one blue, but the two, both his eyes were brown and not blue.

This frightened them all and they began to fall on the floor and cover their eyes and cry. And they cried and they cried and they tried not to cry but it frightened them so to see his two eyes brown and not one brown and one blue that they just cried and cried and cried and cried. And they stopped crying and looked up with their eyes all swollen with crying they almost commenced again because it was true each one had been crying so that now no, their two eyes were not one brown and one blue but they were all blue all their eyes were blue all through. It sounds funny but it is true. And so there was no one of them except the mother Una who had one eye brown and one eye blue and it is funny but it is true.

And after that when each one of the children had their clothes and their ties they could match their eyes and when they had their birthday cake, the cake and the icing could be all blue and if they closed one eye to cut their cake there was no mistake because either eye was blue.

This is all true.

Ursula and United.

Well Ursula said United.

And they said what.

And she said United States.

And they said what.

And she said United States of America.

That was because Ursula was tall and that was not all, Ursula was tall and she was born in a state of the United States of America.

Was she born in a state.

Well let us not state what state.

Because Ursula did not know.

She just did not know.

She did not know in which state of the United States of America she was born she just did not know.

Nobody told her so but she just did not know.

Very well she just did not know.

She liked to count it was Ursula's way so she counted the letters in the alphabet and she counted the letters in the word birthday but she did not like to count the number of states in the United States of America because if she should make a mistake she might you know, she was almost always right when she counted but she might make a mistake and if she did make a mistake and she did not count right she might leave out in her count the state in which she was born and if she left out that state and she did not know which state it was anyway well then she could never have a birthday if that state had been left out and she began to pout and went away. So it was not easy for Ursula to say why she would not count the states in the United States when she loved to count and she counted everything else in every way.

But there it was it was because she did not know in which state of the United States she was born and she could never say.

And there she was one day and she was in a desperate way and she just felt she had to do it today, she just did have to count the states in the United States today.

So she began.

How many states were there anyway and why could not she say in what state she was born just why could not she say.

Well it was a funny reason it was a season when there was a storm when she was born and they were riding along that is her mother and her father were riding along in a boat on a river and they were coming under a bridge and there was a storm and suddenly there was a storm and suddenly Ursula was born and nobody could say in which state they were anyway, four states came together just that way and where was Ursula born, poor dear Ursula she used to say when they asked her in school where she was born she used to say I cannot say and then they all thought it was a funny way to be born and it was.

She knew she had a birthday that was all she could say and she got sadder and sadder and she wanted to be gladder and gladder so one day she ran away, she ran away and she found a boat and she took it away and she went looking around on the water every way to find the place she was born so she could say I was born in a state as well as on a day, and she asked her way and she asked every way and she could not find out and at last she saw a man who was stout sitting in a boat and she commenced to tell him what it was all about. Oh sure he said I remember that storm I remember that day the day you were born and I can say you bet I can say just exactly the day just exactly the storm just exactly the way just exactly the place you were born. Sure I can, come away come away and I'll show you the way.

And he did and there it was the place where she was born and she said in a great state is it a state or is it not a state this spot where I was born.

Of course it's a state said the man who was stout and had pointed it out of course it's a state it is the state of Illinois.

Oh said Ursula oh it is the state of Illinois oh joy oh joy I was born in Illinois oh joy oh joy.

And there it was and she could go home and when they said to her in what state were you born she could say Illinois oh joy oh joy and she would never go away she would never stay away from the state where she was born because it made her nervous to think it might shrink or might go away oh no she would always stay and have a birthday in the state in which she was born.

And now she could count the states of the United States every day and when she came to Illinois she would say oh joy oh joy because Illinois was the state in which she was born and in which every year she had her birthday and so she did not get sadder and sadder but gladder and gladder.

And this is the story of Ursula and United and the end of the U's.

V is Van Virgil Valeska and Very.

Van can a man.

What will **V**an do.

What will he do.

He do.

Van can a man.

Van was his name but all the same he had another name. His name was Papa Woojums spelled like this and when he said it he meant it. Fortunately not.

What.

Not.

Forget me not.

That is Papa Woojums' name.

No one was to blame.

What

Not.

Forget me not.

Van came.

Van is not the same as a weather vane.

But it is up high all the same, and it is a rooster and it knows why, and knows how to tell the wet from the dry. Oh my.

To come back to Van who has a name the same name all the same.

Please be very careful of it.

If you have a name please be very careful of it.

If your name is Papa Woojums

Please be very careful of it.

This is what happened to it.

Not to Van not to Papa Woojums but to the name.

The name Papa Woojums' name was forget me not.

What What he said.

And the name said.

What what forget me not.

How likely to be in a knot.

Dear forget me not.

And anxious to oblige.

Well this is what happened to the name.

There was Papa Woojums and Mama Woojums and Baby Woojums.

And Papa Woojums said what what, and Mama Woojums said Not Not and Baby Woojums said forget me not.

After that there was no secrecy, Van was his name and he was a man and they called him Papa Woojums, just please just think of that.

And then there was a hill and its name was Virgil.

By that time there was a ham and they called it lamb. Well that was a mistake of course. Lamb is a ram or a sheep or mutton it is not a ham.

But Van well he would not make such a mistake and Virgil is a hill and a hill would not make such a mistake not until he did make such a mistake. It would be lighter to make such a mistake than heavier.

Van then, he is a man.

Virgil till, he is a hill.

No mistake at all about that.

Now what happened

What did happen.

Certainly something did.

By mistake.

And a mistake is mistaken.

Oh yes.

What happened.

It is all very confused but more confused than confusing.

Papa Woojums took a picture of a hill which he will, Virgil.

And on the hill grew forget-me-nots.

Papa Woojums began to cry as he began to try to say forget-me-nots.

Very likely forget-me-nots.

How could a birthday come out of forget-me-nots.

Then there suddenly was a story.

When Van that is Papa Woojums was a little boy.

He was not like other little boys.

He had big teeth that bit.

And he wrote poetry.

When his big teeth bit he wrote a poem and when he wrote a poem his big teeth bit.

He was that kind of a little boy.

He wrote a poem about forget-me-nots.

And as he wrote a poem about forget-me-nots his big teeth bit.

Oh not he wrote oh not a forget-me-not.

If you forget me what will I do I will bite with my big teeth all the way through to you.

And he went on writing a poem.

I am Papa Woojums and I'll climb a hill.

Virgil Virgil Virgil.

And he went on writing a poem.

I have a hill, Virgil, I have forget-me-nots when I will, and I was born not on a hill, no Virgil not a hill I was not born on a hill I was born with teeth that bite tight, on a bed of forget-me-nots which were a delight. I am Papa Woojums I am Van and when I bite well when I do nobody ran they just stood too and said boohoo, look at the forget-me-nots too.

Well it happened just like this.

Anybody who writes poems, do they,

Do they have teeth that bite with all their might.

Do they have hills Virgils,

Do they have forget-me-nots,

Plots forget-me-nots,

Or do they have butter-cups.

It is easy to sigh when you say butter-cups.

It is easy to say oh my when you say butter-cups.

But that is not a poem.

A poem has to have big teeth,

And a poem has to say forget-me-nots.

I do not know why

But this is no lie.

That is what a poem has to do.

And a poem has to have a birthday. How could one know how old a poem is if it never had a birthday.

Van Papa Woojums was always sure that it would be a cure for anybody with measles or mumps to see Papa Woojums bite out a poem with teeth so big and forget-me-nots so blue and who are you and it was true, when anybody had measles or mumps and of course mumps is made of bumps, all Papa Woojums had to do was to bite a poem through through his big teeth and away they would go measles and mumps would go up the hill to Virgil.

All right there is no use saying this is not right. Every poem has a birth-day and now everybody knows how, please bow. That is what Van Papa Woojums would say every day. Just like that. A cat, and a birthday and teeth big teeth and a forget-me-not and what.

Well what.

Nothing.

Just nothing at all.

Remember.

Just nothing at all.

How about it.

Remember

Just Nothing at all.

And yet

It is better yet.

That Van Papa Woojums is there with white hair what do you care,

Well big teeth and forget-me-nots and poems and a birthday.

That is what Van Papa Woojums has to say.

Big teeth and forget-me-nots and poems and a birthday.

Poem. Hoe them, toe them.

On his birthday.

And now Valeska and Very.

Valeska did not know any one.

She said Leave it to me.

But she did not know any one

Not even a little girl.

Very she said Valeska said it is very disagreeable not to know anybody not even a little girl. Very.

Then Valeska began to move mountains and after she moved mountains she began to move oceans and after that she said it is very disagreeable not to know anybody, very disagreeable not to know anybody not even a little girl.

Very.

Valeska said Very because she liked very she liked very very much. She was always saying very. That is what made her move oceans and mountains, so she did say very.

Then she said if an oyster has a pearl why can I not know a little girl.

Then she said because if I say very, then very easily I will not be very much nearer what I very often like to have very nearly better than if it was the very best.

It is so very easy to move oceans and so very easy to move mountains but it is not very easy it is not very easy at all to know a little girl.

The more Valeska thought about knowing a little one the more she was careful to very carefully move oceans and to very carefully move mountains. Then she thought of moving the bed. She said if she moved the bed it would make a noise a very little noise but still a noise. So she did not move the bed.

The bed was very nearly ready to be moved but Valeska did not move the bed.

Then when she was left to herself of course she was always just alone because she never knew anybody not even a very little girl.

Still when she was left to herself she moved all the mountains and all the oceans back to where they were, not completely back to where they were, she was a little careless and they did not go quite back to where they were, she did not mix them up, no not that but they did not go back quite to where they were.

She might have been very sorry but was she was she very sorry.

She said Very.

Now if you are all alone and do not even know a very little girl can you have a birthday. How can you have a birthday if there is nobody there to tell you what day you were born nothing but oceans and mountains and they have been moved around.

Valeska was very much alone she did not know anybody not even a very little girl.

Valeska said Very.

Perhaps it was all for the best.

Perhaps.

Perhaps it was best that Valeska should say Very.

Perhaps.

Perhaps yes perhaps no.

Who knows.

Certainly she did say it.

Certainly she said Very.

It is not certain that she did not have a birthday but it is certain that she did not know anybody not even a very little girl. It is also certain that she said Very.

V is V and W is W.

One piece less or one piece more, less makes V and more makes double V or double v let me see, Very well let me see.

Double you. Double you is two for you.

Very was V and double you is a double of you. You and you.

But really not, what what, no really not, it is a trouble to think double and when double you makes double V and when double v makes double you it is better to be v than u and yet u could be v if it was a trouble to you.

Now you see why very is very necessary.

So now there double you which is double v. Like it or not, what.

W is Wendell and Worry and William and Wife.

W is also ewe a ewe lamb.

Yes.

Well there was Wendell.

Wendell was thin very thin, he was as thin as a pin.

Wendell and Worry. It was a worry to Wendell to be so thin, as thin as a pin.

And then little by little he said he would eat a lamb and when he saw the little lamb and the little lamb looked like a little dog and everybody who saw the little lamb said look at the little lamb you would say it was a little dog, well then there was no way for Wendell to eat the little lamb, so Wendell just kept on being thin thin as a pin. It was a worry to him but he was thin oh dear yes he was thin he was as thin as a pin.

Wendell was thin as a pin and he stuck in.

When he stuck in he also stuck out.

Which would not have been so if he had been stout.

When he stuck out he stuck himself that is easy to see when a pin sticks in and sticks out anybody can stick themselves on that pin when they are not careful what they are about.

Wendell did worry about being stout, he said if he were stout he would not be thin and if he were not thin he would not be a pin and if he were not a pin he would not stick out and if he did not stick out what would it all be about.

Well what would it all be about.

It is easy to see that Wendell was that way that everything was a worry to him.

Then he began to think about fishes.

You can catch fishes with a bent pin attached to a string and did oh did Wendell think if he bent double like a bent pin and he tied a string to himself did he think then that he could catch fish which was his wish.

Did he.

He worried about that.

There was so much to worry Wendell and he worried about that.

Perhaps he would go on getting thin perhaps he would get thinner than a pin and what is thinner than a pin, nothing, and so if Wendell became thinner than a pin what would he become nothing, nothing.

Anybody can see that that would be a worry to him.

He would look at a pin hole and see if he could steal in and hide himself in a pin hole, why not if he was as thin as a pin but as he was a boy he was larger than a pin so although he could get in he stuck out and if he stuck out what was it all about.

They might step on him thinking he was a pin but such a long pin that they did not know what it was about.

You can easily understand that everything was a worry to him.

And so as he was sticking in and out of his pin hole, he saw William William and his wife as large as life and William saw him, and William said to his wife when he saw Wendell, this should be a lesson to him, it should be a lesson to him not to be as thin as a pin.

That was easy for William, William was stout so there was nothing for William to worry about.

But William was kindly even if he was stout and even if he said to his wife, it should be a lesson to Wendell not to be as thin as a pin, so he decided to help Wendell out of the pin hole which he was in and out of which he was sticking.

So William went to help Wendell out and he caught hold of him to pull him out of the pin hole he was in, and naturally enough when William who was stout took hold of Wendell who was thin as a pin Wendell stuck into him and William let out a shout and he said what is it about and he said Wendell who was as thin as a pin had stuck into him. And William's wife said let it be a lesson to you William never to catch hold of any one as thin as a pin.

But since Wendell though he was as thin as a pin was as long as a boy there was no way for William to go away because Wendell was stuck right through him.

So there they were William was like a butterfly stuck through with a pin and it did him no good to cry because he was stuck through the whole of him by Wendell who was as thin as a pin and Wendell was still in his pin hole and the only one free was the wife of William and all she could see was that it should be a lesson to them, just be a lesson to them not to be so thin not to be so stout not to be so ready to shout not to be so ready to go about. In short it should be a lesson to them.

So they began to sink down, Wendell like a bent pin and William on top of him and the wife of William dancing around them and crying it should be a lesson to them it should be a lesson to them and Wendell was worrying, because to be a bent pin was a bad thing but if William was on top of him there would be nothing left of him not even a pin hole oh dear.

And then it was queer, just opposite where all this was was a laundry and they were washing clothes and they were hanging them out with clothespins, and William's wife rushed over there she took a clothespin and she rushed back to Wendell and William and she took hold of Wendell with the clothespin and she pulled him out of the pin hole, now they were out of the pin hole, but they were still stuck together as Wendell who was thin as a pin had gone right through William who was stout, and William's wife said, it should be a lesson to him not to be so thin, it should be a lesson to him.

Now what should they do.

Well William's wife had an idea, now they were clear of the pin hole she took the clothespin and she took hold of Wendell she took hold of him with the clothespin and she pulled him through William all the way through and now there was nothing to do because Wendell was not in William any more and William had a hole in him the size of a pin but since William was stout that did not count. Oh dear no.

So.

Well so well so.

What could they do next.

William's wife said it should be a lesson to them but was it.

So then they thought they would fill up the pin hole in William but with what.

And then just opposite was a window and in the window was a cake and the cake was a birthday cake. William's wife saw it first and she said let us take it away and melt the icing first and pour it into the hole and then melt the candles and then seal up the ends and then nobody will know that William had a pin hole in him.

Well that was the way they saved the day.

Wendell who was thin as a pin made his way in into the window he could just creep in, it worried him lest the window should close on him, because even a pin can be smashed flat and thin, but he got in and then he got out and William who was stout was waiting for him with his pin hole all through him. And then they worked all day and William's wife melted the icing and Wendell who was so thin was worried lest they should spill it so he poured it in, and they melted a candle and filled up one end and they melted the icing and poured it in, and when it was all in, they melted the candles and filled the end in and now nobody could tell by looking at him that William had ever been stuck all through with a pin.

And then well then William said it would be a lesson to them, and still there was that birthday cake and even if they had melted all the icing and candles they might as well eat the cake. That was William. Naturally being stout he knew what he was about when cake was around, and even Wendell who was as thin as a pin he could eat birthday cake even though it did make him ache because he was so thin and that was a worry to him and William's wife ate the cake too, she said it should be a lesson to them to the ones that made the cake not to leave it standing where anybody could get in, beside said William's wife they would have cut it with a knife which would have hurt the birthday cake, but we just first melted everything and we did not hurt anything, and anyway said William it ought to be a lesson to them.

And now X.

X is difficult, and X is not much use and it is kind of foolish that X should have been put into the alphabet, it almost makes it an elephant.

X is Xantippe and Xenophon and Xylophone and Xmas.

Xantippe and grip her and Xenophon.

There is no use in saying that Xenophon did not know Xantippe because he did. How else could they both have commenced with X, how else.

X is funny anybody knows that it is funny even X itself knows it is funny.

Xantippe and Xenophon.

And then perhaps it was the letter X perhaps it was but anyway all of a sudden Xantippe did not seem real to Xenophon and Xenophon did not seem real to Xantippe.

Xantippe and grip her and Xenophon could get no grip on Xantippe and Xantippe could not get any grip on Xenophon.

So what did they do. They thought they would part with the letter X. First Xantippe thought she would and then Xenophon. But if they quit the letter X if they lost it like they might a stick which they threw away after a dog had bitten it in play if they did what would happen then then they would be Antippe and Enophon and somehow they felt then as if nobody would ever any more pay them any attention. They knew then that it was the X and not the then that made everybody pay attention to them.

So they just had to begin again and have X where it had been and they just had to be Xantippe and Xenophon even if Xantippe was not real to Xenophon and Xenophon was not real to Xantippe.

So they started over again, X to X, Xantippe to Xenophon.

And what happened then. Well this happened then, they saw five men and ten women and the ten women and the five men walked behind them walked behind Xantippe and Xenophon.

Xantippe and Xenophon knew they were there but they could not look at them because if they looked at them then the X in Xantippe and the X in Xenophon might frighten the ten women and the five men and if the X's

frightened them they might try to kill them. When people are frightened this does happen and Xantippe knew this and so did Xenophon.

What could they do then.

Of course it was all the fault of the X's but they had tried to do without them and that did not suit either of them.

What could they do now, if it were true of you that you were Xantippe or you were Xenophon now what could you do.

Well truly really truly, you could not do anything, you could just wait for something and when something was nothing and nothing was something, then Xantippe and Xenophon were nothing and something.

It was very discouraging and there were the ten women and the five men following, they were always following them.

So then they thought of something, they thought they would change the X in Xantippe for the X in Xenophon, that might help them. So they immediately went to work to exchange them, they changed the X in Xenophon for the X in Xantippe and they did it quickly and completely and then they went on walking, but no the five men and the ten women were still behind them following them, so exchanging one X for the other X had not made it impossible to recognize them not at all, not either one of them not either Xantippe or Xenophon.

So once more that was all and they began to be afraid they would fall and the five men and the ten women would catch them. It was frightening, it did frighten Xantippe and Xenophon.

And if the five men and ten women never went away how could Xantippe and Xenophon stay anywhere that day.

So they thought they would try again to change everything, they thought they would change the birthday of Xenophon for the birthday of Xantippe and that would so change them being born another day would change any one, they thought that this would so change them that no one would know that they were Xenophon and Xantippe Xantippe and Xenophon and the five men and ten women would then go away.

Not at all.

They knew the five men and ten women they knew that Xantippe and Xenophon were Xantippe and Xenophon even if they had changed their birthdays and the five men and ten women kept coming after them and Xantippe and Xenophon did not know what to do and they did not know what to say.

So it happened all of a sudden, the five men and ten women they walked so quickly they walked right into Xenophon and Xantippe and as they walked into them all five of them the men and all ten of them the women opened their mouths as if they were yawning and just then Xenophon and Xantippe disappeared down the mouths of them and no one ever saw Xantippe and Xenophon again and the ten women and five men went away.

And now we have Xylophone and Xmas.

Every one knows what a Xylophone is well does every one. You tap on it and it makes a noise well so does any one.

And X stands for Christmas well any would would any one.

A Xylophone wishes it was the best of all because if it was the best of all it would be given for Christmas. Christmas is so confused, it knows perfectly well perfectly well that there is an X in Christmas and still there it is when there is something to sell there it is there is an X in Christmas.

It is very confusing not at Christmas when there is something to sell but when it is just Christmas that is Christmas.

It is very confusing, why should there be an X in Christmas when there is no X in Christmas why should there be one and why should the Xylophone not be the best of all when when they sell them and they spell them with an X at Christmas.

Life is very confusing said the Xylophone to his Mrs.

Very very confusing said Xmas to Christmas.

There is not much use in a Xylophone being a Xylophone said the Xylophone to his Mrs., not much consolation said the Xylophone not much consolation because the X is not a C no consolation for me said the Xylophone to his Mrs. even if Christmas is Xmas. He can turn a C into an X but a Xylophone a Xylophone can not turn an X into a C.

So why be why be why be.

Why be he, why be a Xylophone.

A Xylophone.

Oh dear me.

So the Xylophone made a groan and his Mrs. thought a thought she thought she would give the Xylophone a C for Christmas and so the C would not be only a consolation to a Christmas but it would also be a consolation for the Xylophone.

You see where the C comes in.

It comes in in comes and in consolation.

So the Mrs. of the Xylophone thought Christmas would be an occasion to give a C to the Xylophone.

Now that seemed all right but was it all right.

It was not all right and the reason it was not all right was this.

In the first place nobody wanted a Xylophone for Christmas and if nobody wanted a Xylophone for Christmas how could the Mrs. of the Xylophone afford to give the Xylophone a C for Christmas.

And then the Mrs. of the Xylophone, well she was very tempted she really was she thought well she thought she would steal she just thought she would she just thought she would steal, yes there is no other word to use for it she would just steal the C from Christmas to give it to the Xylophone. After all at Christmas Christmas did not need a C it was always using an X and when the poor Xylophone whom nobody wanted to buy for Christmas wanted the C for a consolation what harm would it do to steal it from Christmas.

Well Christmas did not feel that way about it not at all, it wanted its X and it wanted its C and nobody so Christmas thought nobody nobody could expect it to give or lend or have stolen from it its C. What was it going to do all year with only an X and not a C. Oh dear me. Anybody could see that it was not possible for Christmas to do without both its X and its C oh dear me.

So Christmas sat up and said no when the Mrs. of the Xylophone tried so quietly to come in and steal its C away to give it to the Xylophone who wanted it for consolation. No said Christmas no, no no. I need my X and I need my C go away and do not bother me with the Xylophone, nobody wants a Xylophone nobody nobody, nobody wants a Xylophone so what difference is it if it only has an X and not a C for consolation.

It seemed hard of Christmas but Xmas did write it on a card Christmas does, Xmas always writes everything on a card Christmas always does and Christmas wrote to the Xylophone go away and leave me alone nobody wants a Xylophone.

It was hard nobody wanted a Xylophone and the Xylophone's Mrs. could not find one not a solitary C as consolation for the poor Xylophone.

So they started to go home alone the Xylophone and the Mrs. of the Xylophone and as they were bumping along, well the Xylophone did make a tune, and somebody was following them, and they turned around and when they found it was a little boy following them they turned away.

And then they heard the little boy say I like that Xylophone please play I wish I had a Xylophone for my birthday.

Well said the Mrs. of the Xylophone what will you give if we give you one for your birthday. What do you want said the little boy I have no money with which to pay but I would love to have a Xylophone for my birthday. Oh said the Xylophone what I want is a C I want a C for consolation and to be like Christmas who has a C and an X and is always such a great success.

So the little boy said my name is Charlie King and you can have a C

or a K either one or both of them if I can have a Xylophone for my birthday. Not a K said they not a K but a C oh yes a C we will take the C from Charlie and here is the Xylophone for your birthday.

And the little boy handed them the C from Charlie and rushed away with the Xylophone for his birthday to play it all day all the day of his birthday.

And Mr. and Mrs. Xylophone went on their way and they were too happy to play the Xylophone because now they had their consolation, they had an X and they had a C just like Christmas and so even on Christmas they had nothing to say except isn't it a lovely evening.

The end of the X's.

Yvonne and You, Yes and Young.

These are the Y's why not.

What, what not.

Oh my.

There is a difference between the beginning and the end if there is nothing to mend.

That is why the Y is always comfortable enough, comfortable enough.

Yvonne and you.

Yvonne was a girl.

She was the youngest of five, perhaps she was the youngest of six, perhaps she was the youngest of seven.

Anyway she was the youngest yet, perhaps that was the reason her name was Yvonne Yet.

There was another family and their name was not Yet it was Young and the next to the youngest one was named Yes Young. Yes that was his name Yes Young, and he could guess that Yvonne Yet would let him come.

Which he did.

What a pleasant day that was for Yvonne Yet, and Yes Young.

They do have funny names around there.

That is natural enough that they have funny names around there if you do not like Y.

Natural enough if they do not like Y around there and they do not like Y. Why, well they just do not like Y. Not well enough not to be shy when they see any one whose name begins with Y.

So what could they do with these two, Yvonne Yet and Yes Young, they were just too full of Y's to get along with any one living around there.

Anyway Yes Young was a policeman and he was marrying he said he was Yvonne Yet.

Yvonne Yet's father and mother, mother and father were sailors.

Yes Young's father and mother and mother and father were bakers.

Yes Young's father and mother baked for sailors, and Yvonne Yet's father and mother sailed for bakers so it was natural enough for Yvonne Yet and Yes Young to get along, particularly as she had been the youngest and he had been next to the youngest, and so they did get along and they were young and strong and the letter Y had not gotten them yet no not yet, yes not yet, you bet.

So there they were married Yvonne Yet and Yes Young and it did not do anybody any harm. Yes Young was a policeman, even if his father and mother did the baking and Yvonne Yet stayed at home even though her father and mother were sailors and were sailing.

So there they were married and they did not have any trouble with the letter Y yet, yes not yet.

Pretty soon the trouble with the letter Y was going to begin.

They heard some one sing and this is the song he sang.

Imagine he sang imagine if you can

Imagine said he and as he said it he sang imagine if you can

What you could plan

Imagine he sang imagine if you can how much it would cost to get back a letter if it could be lost. Imagine that if you can, and his voice rose higher and higher imagine if you can is what he sang if you began to have a name and not a letter for the same.

Imagine that he said and when he said it he sang imagine that if you can.

Yvonne Yet and Yes Young were there, it was an afternoon and everybody was sitting around in a crowd when suddenly this man began to sing and he sang imagine it if you can.

Yvonne looked at Yes and Yes looked at Yvonne. They remembered they had put the letter Y in an envelope and now where was it. Oh dear they said what a mess. Y is certainly the one not to be taken along and others have two letters one different from the other and a husband and a wife they have a different father and a mother so they cannot not have this bother but we oh dear me, Y Y Y Y oh why are we only Y oh why oh why, and they cried so loud that the man who was singing stopped singing just to hear them say Y oh why oh why oh why only Y.

It is sweet said the man singing it is sweet and it is neat to have the letters A to Z but not the letter Y. Why not the letter Y. Oh my.

Well it is a very funny story that, why not the letter Y.

The letter Y you see the letter Y is in an envelope and when it falls into the fire it burns. Now if a letter burns then it is not there. Believe it or not it is true.

Now the letter Y was put into an envelope they remembered that and the envelope was put into the fire, that is what happened to the letter Y. Of course that is what happened to the letter Y and that is because it is in cry and in Oh my, that is the reason why the letter Y was put into an envelope, and into the fire and the envelope was all burned up and in the ashes there were no sashes there was nothing at all, the letter Y was gone.

It was a very sad story.

And there were Yvonne Yet and Yes Young and they just did not know what to say.

Yvonne could not say to Yes what do you think Yes because there was no letter Y and Yes Young could not say to Yvonne I will take care of you Yvonne because the letter Y was burned away, away away away.

And the worst of it all was that Yes Young was a policeman, now a policeman should have seen to it that the letter Y was not put into the envelope and even if it was put into an envelope it should not have been put into the fire and if it was put into the fire the fire should have been put out before the envelope was burnt up.

Yes Young was a policeman and that is what he should have done. Yes Young.

Well it was a very sad day.

Those are sad days when a letter the only letter that can make you know that you are you is burned away. Oh dear a very sad day.

And what did they say.

Well Yes Young was a policeman and he said it is an awful thing but I will find a way, and Yvonne Yet looked at him and said do you think you can do anything, and that I will not have to go away. Not yet, was all Yes Young could find to say.

But he went away to do something.

The first thing he saw was the dog Never Sleeps and he said if he never sleeps perhaps he can help me find something that will take the place of the letter Y's and so he called Never Sleeps and Never Sleeps and Was Asleep woke up and came with him. He told them what he wanted and they said well I know what to do, I know a baby is going to be born and they are going to call it Yvonne, now it does not make any difference to that baby if they call it Lucy instead of Yvonne because it is just born. Now we will call out Lucy Lucy and the baby will cry and they will all say oh my and perhaps Lucy is a prettier name than Yvonne and that will be Lucy's birthday and so there will be an Yvonne for Yvonne Yet and so well she is not a baby but if it is her birthday perhaps it will be just the same.

Well that was a fine idea and they carried it through and Never Sleeps and Was Asleep cried Lucy Lucy, Baby Baby, Baby Lucy, Baby Lucy, and everybody said of course we will call baby who has just been born we will call her Lucy and not Yvonne. So with the Y from Yvonne the policeman Yes Young went home.

Well it was Yvonne Yet's birthday, so whatever you say she was pleased to have it be that way.

But and she began to cry no matter how I try I can not stay with Yes Young because his letter Y was all burned away, you have not found another one she said to Yes Young. Not yet, said the policeman Yes Young I have only just begun.

So off he went again and he thought that Never Sleeps and Was Asleep were police dogs, well they were not, they were just little brown dogs but when a policeman called them they did come.

So they said they would find Yes or Young.

But there were none.

All the Young wanted Young and all the Yes wanted Yes.

So what could a policeman do, Not yet said the policeman but that was all he could do.

And then one day there on the door he saw a sign which said Yes Young. It was an empty house it was to let and he said how could that say Yes Young. Well it was this way. One day, girls and boys were at play, and one of them did say let's play that we are younger every day. And they did they began to play that they were younger every day and one of them had written this up on the door while he was lying on the floor he had written on the door Yes Young.

And Yes Young being a policeman he could go in, and he could take the door down and carry it home to Yvonne and then they were just all right again, Yvonne had had her birthday present of Yvonne and Yes Young a policeman had carried away a Yes Young. And so they were very careful after that of the Y's, they never said Oh my and they never said cry and they never said try, they just went on being Yvonne and Yes Young, and they never said Not yet, never, never never. And so they lived happily ever after and had a great many children but they never gave them any name that began with Y not one.

And now it is Z.

Z is not the last but one it is the last one.

Zebra and Zed, Zoology and Zero.

Z is a nice letter, I am glad it is not Y, I do not care for Y, why, well that is the reason why, I do not care for Y, but Z is a nice letter.

I like Z because it is not real it just is not real and so it is a nice letter nice to you and nice to me, you will see.

Zebra and Zed.

A Zebra is a nice animal, it thinks it is a wild animal but it is not it goes at a gentle trot. It has black and white stripes and it is always fat. There never was a thin Zebra never, and it is always well as sound as a bell and its name is Zebra.

It is not like a goat, when a goat is thin there is nothing to do for him, nothing nothing, but a Zebra is never thin it is always young and fat, just like that.

Well there was a little French girl named Zed, she said her name was Zed and it was her name and everybody called her by the same. She was a little French girl and she had a father, her father was not fat he was thin, he was an explorer and if you explore and explore you have to be able to go through any door to explore and so you just have to be thin.

But Zed was not so thin she was quite fat and her father the explorer always brought home for her something especial for her birthday that came from far away.

So Zed said, she held her head, that was because she was not thin but fat and she leaned her head her heavy fat head on her father who was thin and she said father what will you bring me for my birthday and he said what shall I bring, and she said I want a Zebra because he is never thin, I want a Zebra for my birthday.

So her father the explorer went away and he did not forget her birthday, and he did not forget her Zebra and it was easy to get a Zebra because they are always young and fat and they think they are wild but they are not. So it was very easy to catch him the Zebra for Zed's birthday, but Zed was to have her birthday far away and how was her father the explorer to get the Zebra there for her on her birthday.

Well there was no boat there, that with any amount of care could get the Zebra there for Zed's birthday she was having her birthday too far away.

And Zed just had to have her Zebra for her birthday she just had to have it on that day there was nothing else to say she just had to have it on that day otherwise she would hold her head all day. Zed was that way.

So her father the explorer looked around and this was what he found an airplane and he thought if it sailed away in a day it would bring the Zebra to Zed for her birthday.

So the first thing to do was to paint the airplane so it looked like a Zebra too, not red and blue but white and black and in stripes to look like a back.

So that is what the father of Zed started to do he painted the airplane until it looked exactly like a Zebra so when the Zebra was asked to come too, he would think it was a Zebra asking him to come which would be fun and he would come with a run.

Which he did.

There he was on the airplane and now the fun had begun, but in a very little while the Zebra would know that the airplane was all alone it and the Zebra and Zebras like a lot of Zebras around to paw the ground and to be Zebras together and to sound like Zebras and not to be alone, if Zebras are alone they make a moan and say they are not Zebras, and if they say they are not Zebras they are not Zebras and so there would be no use in taking a Zebra to Zed for her birthday if when he got there he was not a Zebra at all, that would not do at all not at all.

So Zed's father thought hard and he decided to paint the clouds and the sky like Zebras black and white stripes, so that as the Zebra sailed past he would say yes at last there are nothing but Zebras all around, it is like the ground all covered with Zebras and I am not alone and so I will not groan but be a Zebra and my black and white stripes will last.

So Zed's father went to work he was in an airplane ahead and he painted so fast the sky and the clouds that as the Zebra's plane came sailing along, the Zebra saw nothing but Zebras around, because even the ground Zed's father the explorer had painted black and white in a stripe like the Zebra, so the Zebra sailed along and never knew he was not there where he had been born with nothing but Zebras everywhere and so he came down to be taken there where they were to prepare that he would not groan because he was alone.

Little fat Zed from her feet to her head was a Zebra, and the house and the trees and even the breeze was painted black and white stripes like a Zebra, so the Zebra was happy to stay and it was her birthday and all that day and all every day she and the Zebra passed in play, they were young and they were fat and that was that and her father the explorer went away to explore some more and to begin again on Zed's next birthday.

Zoology.

Zoology oh dear what is Zoology.

Zoology is all about wild animals thin and stout and they do all shout we are Zoology that is what Zoology is about.

Well once upon a time there was a little thing, he was a dog his name was Never Sleeps and he had a brother Was Asleep and they always were together.

A big dog likes to be with a little dog and a little dog likes to be with a big dog.

That is because it is so flattering for the big dog to have the little dog admire him and for the little dog to be allowed to come with a big dog. Boys are like that and girls are like that, they like a little one to say how big they are and they like a big one to say how little they are. Never Sleeps and Was Asleep were not like that, Was Asleep was asleep and Never Sleeps was awake otherwise they were twins.

Now Never Sleeps when he was not asleep and he never was asleep heard a little boy there was a little boy there and there were three little girls that made four and no more, the little boy was reading a book about Zoology, and at first Never Sleeps however he could try did not understand why the little boy was reading a book about Zoology but pretty soon he heard him tell how dogs just little dogs like Never Sleeps, could be dogs that chased and tore that rushed around not on a floor but in the woods and far away and killed everything that was in their way. Most exciting is what Never Sleeps did say, most exciting.

So he tried to wake Was Asleep but there was no use in that, and there was no use in trying to wake the cat so all alone he went away to be the way the dogs had been before they had been a twin like he was with Was Asleep, just a dog to sleep by night and by day.

Zoology was exciting.

Up to then the worst thing Never Sleeps had ever done was to run to bark and to tear the clothes of those he chose as the ones he loved, he tore their clothes when he was afraid they would go away and leave him there to stay and bark and cry away, and he tore their clothes when he wanted them to come away and he tore their clothes when anything frightened him and being a brave dog, Never Sleeps was a brave dog why anything could frighten him, that is what a brave dog is, and that is the reason everybody can love them because anything can frighten them.

So that is what Zoology was it was frightening, it was frightening for the animals being it all the wild animals and all the tame ones because anything could frighten them and it was frightening to anyone reading about them because anybody reading about them would not know that anything could frighten the wild animals and the tame ones that make Zoology but anything can, thunder and lightning and sun and rain and heat and cold and fog and a train, and other animals and men and even children and women, well that is very nice to know it makes everybody feel brave to know that anything can frighten anybody so.

And Never Sleeps was like that, not Was Asleep, because he was asleep and as he was not frightened by being asleep and he always was asleep he was never awake long enough to be frightened or to frighten.

But Never Sleeps was not like that, he liked to think he was stronger than a cat or a bird or the moon or coming too soon.

So then one day after he had heard all that Zoology had to say he went out to frighten something, not to be frightened but to be frightening. So he went along and he saw a door and he had never noticed that door before and it was a little open. So he put his nose in and a paw and then the door opened a little more and he went in.

And there in the dark corner sat a hen and beneath her were the eggs she was hatching to give all twelve little chickens their birthday.

Well when Never Sleeps saw her in the dark on the floor he barked as he never had barked before and he put forward a paw and he knew he was frightened and a little frightening, and he was right because the hen although he had given her a fright knew what to do all right, she rushed at him her wings drumming, and fire like lightning shooting out from one eye and then her other eye, and oh my, the door was shut or shutting and what could Never Sleeps do, or the hen too and all the twelve baby chickens waiting for their birthday.

Just then, well just then there was a moo there was a cow too and she did not like what everybody was doing and Never Sleeps was frightened by that and there was a cat and there was a goat and there was a sheep but there was no boat and oh dear there was no coat to hide in. Well anyway some way

Never Sleeps never knew how he was out of the door and he said not ever any more would he listen to Zoology, Zoology was too much, he preferred Was Asleep and the boy but Never Sleeps when the boy was asleep took the book of Zoology and tore it in two and chewed it all through, he had had enough of Zoology enough and some more. And then there in the dark in the corner on the floor the hen went on as before and the twelve little chickens they certainly had and they were glad they had, they had their birthday on that day, and it was peaceful too and the cow said moo and the goat was there and a chair and a sheep to keep and a cat so fat and that was that.

And Never Sleeps was far away and he just had nothing to say that day.

And now it is Zero.

Oh dear oh Zero.

Zero they said and they felt well fed.

Oh hero dear oh Zero.

Oh hear oh dear oh Zero.

So Zero is a hero

And why is Zero a hero.

Because if there was no Zero there would not be ten of them there would only be one.

And if there was no Zero there would not be a hundred of them there would only be one.

So Zero is a hero.

And if there was no Zero there would not be a thousand of them there would only be one.

And if there was no Zero there would not be ten thousand of them there would only be one.

And if there was no Zero there would not be a hundred thousand of them there would only be one.

So Zero is a hero.

And if Zero was not a hero there would not be a million of them there would only be one.

And if Zero was not a hero if he was not a real hero there would not be a billion of them there would only be one one single one.

And if Zero was not a hero well if Zero was not a hero how could anything be begun if there was only one one one.

So Zero is a hero and as Zero is a hero there are ten of them and each one of them has a birthday instead of only one.

It would be sad to be all alone every birthday so that is what they all say the ten and the hundred and the thousand and the ten thousand and the hundred thousand and the million and the billion they say oh Zero dear Zero oh hear oh we say that thanks to the Zero the hero Zero we all have a birthday.

Hurray.

And so that is all there is to say these days about Alphabets and Birthdays and their ways.